T0159158

Return to
Mariah

FLARRY W. HENRY, III

authorHOUSE®

AuthorHouse™
1663 Liberty Drive
Bloomington, IN 47403
www.authorhouse.com
Phone: 1-800-839-8640

© *2015 Flarry W. Henry, III. All rights reserved.*

*No part of this book may be reproduced, stored in
a retrieval system, or transmitted by any means
without the written permission of the author.*

*This is a work of fiction. All of the characters, names, incidents,
organizations, and dialogue in this novel are either the products
of the author's imagination or are used fictitiously.*

Published by AuthorHouse   2/2/2015

ISBN: 978-1-4969-5418-3 (sc)
ISBN: 978-1-4969-5417-6 (e)

*Any people depicted in stock imagery provided by Thinkstock are models,
and such images are being used for illustrative purposes only.
Certain stock imagery © Thinkstock.*

This book is printed on acid-free paper.

*Because of the dynamic nature of the Internet, any web addresses or
links contained in this book may have changed since publication and
may no longer be valid. The views expressed in this work are solely those
of the author and do not necessarily reflect the views of the publisher,
and the publisher hereby disclaims any responsibility for them.*

CONTENTS

Part 1 - Worlds Apart

Part 2 - Standing At The Crossroads

Part 3 - Trials, Tribulations And Judgment Day

In memory of Girard Carlos Henry

PART 1

WORLDS APART

CHAPTER 1

Isn't that Right, Sheriff Solomon?

Filling in for a sick deputy and taking on the midnight patrol was a welcomed change of pace for Sheriff Angela Solomon. Chief in command of her small, eight-member police department in rural Mariah, North Carolina, it had been years since Angela had gone out on a routine patrol. Starting the twelve o'clock shift, the chill outside felt unreal, especially after such a hot midsummer day. Nonetheless, tonight was going to be a welcome break from the usual, dull office routine of sitting behind a desk all day.

Despite the weird cool weather, it was quiet and peaceful, just how Angela liked it. Routine, but relaxing. Then, patrolling on the outskirts of town, she was startled by an unusual black murkiness that seemed to appear out of nowhere, hindering her vision. She began to be alarmed when the thick, black fog quickly engulfed her car. Ever the professional, she checked the time on the dash. It was exactly one o'clock in the morning.

Suddenly, directly in front of her, a wrecked SUV, upside down, emerged from the fog, forcing Angela to swerve radically, just missing the wreck, Stunned, she pulled her cruiser over to the side of the road. She looked back, but was unable to see a thing due to the thick fog. She got on the radio.

"Harriett, this is Sheriff Solomon calling in, do you read?"

"I'm here, Sheriff. What's up?"

"I'm reporting a bad accident located north of town on Oak Leaf Road, just past Benton Creek. You had better send an emergency response team, and we are going to need Jimmy's tow truck. There is a wrecked vehicle blocking the road. Take caution coming out in this fog. Probably caused the accident. It is so heavy, I almost crashed into the vehicle myself. How bad is it there, Harriett? Over."

"What fog? There are no reports of fog over this way, Sheriff. It's is as clear as a bell. Over."

"Really? Weird…. Nonetheless—"

"Don't worry—the team is as good as on its way. I'll give them a heads up about the fog you got over there, Sheriff. Over."

"Great, Harriet. Thanks. I'm going to check the accident for casualties. Stand by. Out."

Looking around, surrounded by the strange fog, Angela wondered, *What is up with this weird weather?*

Angela grabbed her flashlight and got out of the car to investigate the scene. Walking over to the overturned SUV submerged in the fog and smoke, she detected a strange sulfuric odor lingering with the burnt metal and gasoline fumes. She touched the rear end of the still-hot vehicle. Checking the license plates, she gasped, realizing it belonged to her two close friends, John and Debbie Davidson. In a panic, she ran around to the front of the overturned wreck, dreading what she might find, but knowing on some level that it wasn't going to be good. The partially burned bodies of her friends were still strapped in, upside down, like some horror movie amusement park ride. Even as her knees buckled in shock and grief, Sheriff Solomon's cop brain wondered if they might have been thrown free of the wreck had they forgotten to put on their seat belts.

Nearby, a strange, muffled moan drifted out from the dark swirl of the fog, snapping Angela out of it. She quickly gathered herself. Searching cautiously farther down the road, she located another ruined vehicle. A black Chevy pickup decked out with expensive chrome rims had crashed head-on into a big elm. Both doors were wide open. Hearing the moan again, she swung her flashlight, the beam finding a man with long, gray hair under a cowboy hat, sitting on the side of the road, rocking back and forth. Hunched over, he continued to moan with both hands covering his face. She noted that his moans had a sort of cadence, like a mantra of some type.

"Are you all right, sir? Are you injured?" The sheriff approached the man cautiously.

Startled, he scrambled to get up off the ground. His quick, unexpected move put the sheriff on guard. His back still turned, he cleared his throat and slowly staggered around to face her. Shining her flashlight in his face, she saw that the elderly man's thick, gray handlebar moustache and beard were soaked in blood, and an old scar sealed one eye. He glared at her in a drunken stupor with his one good eye. He'd jumped up so easily, Angela assumed his only injury to be a broken nose.

"Sir, are you all right? What happened here? Are you alone? Help is on the way."

He squinted at her with the good eye, staggering around, obviously inebriated. Grabbing his nose, he grumbled in pain, smearing his moustache and beard with blood.

"Oh, no.... I'm fine," the old black cowboy mumbled, grumpy and irritated. He paused to look down at the blood dripping on his sharp, black silver-tipped snakeskin boots.

"Aww, *darn* it!" Staggering, holding his nose, he tried to rub his boots off on the back of his pants. Angela wondered how he stayed on his feet. He began to search clumsily on the ground around him.

"Have you seen my hat lying around here anywhere?" he asked.

"Yeah. It's on your head. You have been drinking tonight, huh. Show me your identification, sir."

Covering his bleeding nose with his hand, he reached up and felt his hat. He giggled, and with a wicked grin he snidely responded, "Well, yes, I guess it's pretty damn obvious I have been drinking, Sheriff. That ain't against the law, and I think I broke my freaking nose!"

Angry and exasperated by the drunken man's insensitivity to what was going on, Angela pointed over to the black pick-up truck.

"Were you driving that truck over there?" Angela demanded.

The old drunk reached behind his back.

Drawing her weapon, she shouted, "Freeze, mister! Don't move! Hold it right there!"

"Take it easy, lady! I was just getting a handkerchief for my nose!"

She nodded for him to go ahead, but held on to her service revolver. Slowly, he pulled out the red bandanna for her to see. Covering his broken nose, it cracked loudly as he straightened it out, howling.

"Wow. Okay. Sir? I need to see your driver's license, proof of insurance and registration." She holstered her weapon. He made no attempt to provide identification of any type. Pulling out her ticket booklet and pen, she repeated her prior questions to no avail. The old man just sat, grinning in silence and staring into thin air.

"Okay. That's it. I am placing you under arrest for driving under the influence, hindering a criminal investigation, and suspicion of vehicular manslaughter. Don't you realize that there are two dead people in that vehicle over there? Turn around, put your hands behind your head and interlock your fingers."

Appearing that he could not care any less about what she said or about being arrested, the handcuffed drunk fell into the back of the squad car wearing that audacious smile. He leaned back on the seat and started moaning his weird mantra and rocking.

Losing patience, Angela drew her weapon and glared angrily at the old drunken cowboy. She cocked her revolver, shoving it forcibly against the side of his head.

"Look, fella, you need to start talking about what happened here. Now!" she threatened. He turned to face her. His good eye revealed no signs fear.

"My name is Ezekiel Joppa, and I'd like to see you prove that I was even in that truck. Anyone that was inside that thing should be dead!" He showed his teeth and offered her a low, animal growl.

"Did you just *growl* at me?" she asked. He remained silent, grinning.

"I hope you got a good lawyer, Mr. Joppa, because you are going to need one!" the sheriff said through clenched teeth.

"I ain't going to need no lawyer!" he replied, turning away to hide his smile.

"We'll see about that." She slammed the door.

"Yeah, we'll see about that, all right! Yeah, you are going to see, real soon."

An overbearing stench of alcohol had filled the air in the small space. Angela stepped to the back of her car for a clean breath. Using the hood of the trunk, she finished her ticket and accident report. She looked at her watch, wondering what was keeping the EMTs. Sliding into the front seat, she calls in. "Harriet, it's the Sheriff. It was the Davidsons who were killed in the accident up here. Send Fred and some of the volunteer recruits, and notify the coroner. I have a suspect in custody and there may be others."

* * *

John ambled through the fog, not really registering the oddness of its presence. It seemed to fit with the mood of the night; his date with Faith had been quiet and dreamlike. He thought he must be seeing things when the eerie red light emerged from the murk. As he moved closer, he recognized the emergency lights of the patrol car, muted to soft edges of flashing color. He was close to home, and a feeling of dread coiled through his gut. Getting closer, the SUV materialized. It looked like his parents' car. *Oh God*. Without thinking, he ran up to the burned vehicle, stopped short by shock and horror.

"Noooo! Oh, my God, no, no, please!" John fell to his knees, then, seeming to realize that they might still be alive, he shouted and threw himself at his mother's seat belt, struggling to free her.

Angela heard John's anguished hollering and made her way through the glowing fog in its direction. Recognizing her friends' son, she grabbed hold of him, trying to pull him from the car..

"John! John! They're both gone. John!" She dragged him from the smoldering, gruesome mess.

"Let me go! Get your hands off me!" The sheriff's soothing voice penetrated his panic and the fight began to fall away. "Let me go, Sheriff! Please, I got to get her out. . . . I have to get her out of there!" He collapsed finally in the Sheriff's arms, weeping in sorrowed torment.

"Oh, baby. . . . I'm so sorry, I'm so sorry," she whispered, rocking him. "I am so, so sorry, they are both gone! We can do nothing but pray for them now." Angela wept with the boy.

"Pray?" John, filled with anger and guilt, cried as he struggled in her arms. "I was supposed to … we always go to bible study together on Wednesday night! Tonight I told them no—I wanted to see Faith—oh God!"

Angela grabbed him by the shoulders and turned him around to face her.

"John, I want you to listen to me very carefully. Do not make me have to cuff you. I want you to know that I have a possible suspect in the car."

"What?" John's focus turned immediately to the back of the squad car. Angela felt his muscles tense.

He took a good look at the mumbling, long-haired old man sitting in the back of the car, rocking back and forth, wearing a stupid-looking cowboy hat. The man went still and looked up at John. As they walked toward the squad car, the heavy smell of liquor reached John's nostrils. The old cowboy's broken, bloody nose was still dripping profusely, and he flashed a bloody, crooked-toothed smile at John.

Incensed by the foolish, drunken jester, John exploded into a crazed rage, ready to tear the man's head off with his bare hands. He tried breaking loose from the sheriff's grip. She quickly put him to the ground. Her knee in his back, she pulled both arms behind him, cuffing him with a plastic restraint tie band pulled from her boot. As they struggled, the wind blustered, and the fog began to spin around them.

Getting up off the ground, they backed away as a swirling black ball of mist suddenly swished over their heads, swallowing the squad car in front of them.

The old cowboy's voice echoed through the ominous swirling cloud, leaving a spiteful gibe. "HA HA! I *told* you I wasn't going to need no lawyer! But we will meet again soon, I promise you both!"

Angela and John looked on in disbelief as the black cloud morphed into a flaming ball and vanished into the sky, taking the odd fog with it and leaving the cruiser behind.

"What the hell was that, Sheriff?" John yelled.

"Stay right there!" Angela ordered.

John ignored her and they both rushed over to the squad car, confounded. Only the handcuffs remained, lying shiny and pristine on the empty back seat. It was as if the man had never existed.

"Where is he? What just happened here, Sheriff?" Fear and hysteria squeaked out with his voice.

"I—I don't know! I do not know what to tell you, John. How can I explain something like this?" she replied, mystified. She was not at all accustomed to the feeling.

"Oh, my God, they were coming home from bible study! This cannot be right, Sheriff! I should be over there, dead like them!" He looked up into the night sky. "WHY would You do this to them, why would You take them away from me.… I hate You!" Wailing, the young man collapsed to the asphalt.

* * *

The backup the sheriff'd called for earlier finally arrived on the scene. Her old dependable friend, Deputy Fred Thomas, stepped out of his cruiser.

"Holy! What on earth happened here? Y'all right?"

"Yeah, Fred. I'll get to it. The fog's gone, but my head's still a bit muddled."

"Yeah, about that. It was a clear ride all the way here, Sheriff. Nothing came odd until I got to this here terrible accident. Tow truck is on the way. Is this our suspect?" He jutted a thumb over at John, who was still in restraints.

"No, Fred, he is okay, I had to calm him down." She released John's cuffs. "This is John. His parents, the Davidsons, are the vics."

"Jeez. I'm sorry, kid!" John remained unmoving.

"They were close friends of mine, Fred. The other vehicle is down the road, crashed into a tree."

"What vehicle? I don't see one…." The confused deputy continued to search.

Pointing, she began to make her way to where the pickup had been. It had vanished completely, the elm unmarred.

"Probly a bad time to ask, but…. Harriett mentioned a suspect in custody?" Fred was concerned regarding her obvious state of confusion.

Angela was at a complete loss. Before she could even began to explain, John burst out, "Yeah, Officer, the suspect escaped and went that a way!" John pointed straight up above his head. You had to see that ball of fire when you were pulling up! A deranged cowboy just flew away from here in it!"

John turned to Angela for confirmation. "Isn't that right, Sheriff Solomon?"

CHAPTER 2

La Vie Est Belle (Life Is Beautiful)

Eighteen months later, in the dead of winter four days before Christmas Eve, a strange flaming orb appeared above the small coastal town of Odem, Massachusetts. Wintry night skies abruptly sprung to life. An odd Nor'easter snowstorm unleashed blinding flashes of cracking lightning and sudden tremendous thunderclaps. Bellowing black clouds erupted, producing a spinning, flaming spectacular in mid-air. The blazing phenomenon quickly changed into a disturbing event: emerging from the floating ball of flame, a custom-designed, black 1963 Chevy pickup materialized, a radical paint job of roaring flames covering the hood. Fully tricked out with chrome rims, this ominous paranormal sight marked the appearance of Ezekiel Joppa.

Hovering above in the raging storm, sitting behind the steering wheel with that insouciant grin, he chomped on the end of an unlit cigar butt. His middle finger flamed up, lighting the fat stub. The glare revealed his face, flaky and crinkled and covered by a thick gray moustache and bushy beard. His crooked nose leaned toward a thick keloid scar on the right side of his face where the eye had been. His big, black high-crowned, wide-brimmed cowboy hat was pulled down low to his brows. He was dressed nattily in a long, black leather overcoat and matching leather vest over a white silk shirt. A bolo tie with a fat turquoise stone, and black jeans tucked into black snakeskin boots with silver tips and spurs completed his fancy outfit. He removed the sheriff's badge from his vest coat, putting it in the glove compartment.

Cloaked by the odd Nor' easter flash storm, the Chevy truck began to descend slowly to earth. The truck settled in the woods a few miles outside of town, landing on a deserted back road. The old cowboy took an extra-long drag off his smoke and forcibly exhaled. He mumbled a chant under his breath then slowly fanned his hand in front of him. He pulled out a flask, taking a long swig, and then another long drag, before flipping the cigar butt out the open window. He shouted with glee into the woods surrounding him.

"It's good to be back! Merry Christmas, Ernestine Jackson, my love!"

The tempestuous weather subsided suddenly.

A sly grin cracked his bearded face as he thought about the holiday surprises she was about to receive.

For Ernestine Jackson, however, the storms were just starting. Actually, you could say they began nine months earlier.…

An unfriendly rocky coast snaked the shoreline just outside the town of Odem. It had become her favorite place for peace and comfort. Taking advantage of a rare sunny day, she was enjoying a long walk along the chilly coast, daydreaming. She realized that she was standing in front none other than the Mermaid's Tavern. It was the last place Ernestine would normally patronize, yet there she was, already inside, standing at the bar. Ordering a hot Irish coffee with a double shot of whiskey, she had no idea what had drawn her into this shady place by the docks. She was a seal swimming in a pool of hungry sharks. She felt something evil grab hold inside of her in a place she did not even know existed.

Her order arrived. She took a few sips but, convinced she was not in a safe place, she decided to get the heck out. She paid her coffee tab and, turning to leave, she bumped into a most handsome man. He introduced himself as Thomas Delroy. He captivated the young woman with his good looks, charm and intelligence. She was immediately infatuated.

Later, she would recall the experience. "Something strange took me over that night! Why would I ... I mean, how could I just go to a place like that, meet and get plastered with a complete stranger and so willingly act like such a.... Ooohhh, I am going to say it ... just like some kind of floozy whore! I had had too much to drink, or maybe it was something that I drank that night! It was not my doing!" Something truly had possessed her that night. She'd ended up taking a morning after pill, blaming everything on the alcohol and chalking it up to a girl-gone-wild crazy college night out. Still, she discovered shortly thereafter that she was pregnant by the only man she had ever had sex with. Her first time, a one night stand. Totally depressing. Making a big life decision, Ernestine committed to having the baby and kept it a secret from everyone. She never heard from the father after that night, and part of her felt that was a blessing.

As time passed, Ernestine fell deeper into depression. It was so hard keeping things secret. Her parents knew nothing about the baby and were expecting her to graduate in May. Before she began to show, she faded from the social media scene and stopped hanging out with friends. Eventually, she took a maternity leave from school; she'd miss the winter semester at. She realized that she had to put graduation on hold, which meant her parents were bound to find out and become aware of her situation. They were already getting concerned about the fact that she had not come home for any holiday or during school breaks. Ernestine felt so guilty keeping in touch with only a monthly phone call of brief, shallow conversations. She often lied, using the excuse of schoolwork and her online business taking up most of her time in order to avoid talking much about her personal life.

Life moved along smoothly for the very busy, soon to be single student mom. Because of her solitude, she was able to concentrate on her business full time. With the winter holiday season in full swing, her online greeting card sales were picking up very well.

Ernestine had been a no-show at her parents' that Thanksgiving. She just hadn't had the heart to disappoint them. Unconsciously rubbing her stomach, she thought of how tired she was of making lame apologies about being ill or having to study for a make-up exam. Her mother had called a couple of weeks ago, upset and worried.

"We haven't seen you for almost a year! I know something's wrong. You're a terrible liar. Please, honey. Just talk to me."

Ernestine felt the strongest urge to blurt out the whole story, but she chickened out.

"It's nothing, Mom, really. I'm just so tired busy." Without answering, Mom pulled out the big guns and put her father on the phone.

"That's *it*, Ernie! We are really getting worried. Either you tell me right now you're coming home for Christmas or we're driving to Odem."

"Okay, okay! I promise! I'll come home Christmas break."

Now Christmas was only four days away, and she still had not worked up the courage to tell them.

Three soft taps at the door pulled her from her anxious musings. A happy male voice was singing a cheerful tune through the door.

"La vie est belle . . . life is beautiful!"

Who could that possibly be? she thought.

Apprehension mixed with anticipation as she headed for the door. She squinted through the peephole but couldn't see anyone.

Then a big, black cowboy hat popped up in front of the small hole. She panicked. *Could it be Dad?* It would fit well with his character, showing up wearing a cowboy hat instead of the traditional Santa hat, jokingly doing what concerned fathers do, showing up unannounced surprising their little girls. *Oh my God, how am I ever going to explain this to him?*

"Daddy? Is that you out there, playing around?" She closed her eyes, as if that would help.

"Oh, it's your daddy, all right…. Surprise! It's me, Thomas—Thomas Delroy!"

Ernestine's eyes opened wide with shock. It was baby's father. Here. The last person she wanted to see! Her hand froze on the knob. She was totally freaked out. He tapped lightly on the door again.

"Hey, Ernestine, remember me, baby? It's Thomas!"

"Thomas?" Grimacing, she cracked the door slightly, leaving the chain attached. Yep. That was the face. He stood there, dressed sharply and smiling in her doorway. Her senses suddenly heightened, and she wrapped an arm protectively around her stomach, keeping it hidden behind the door.

"Thomas! What are you doing here?" she asked through the narrowly cracked door, baffled by his cowboy get-up.

"That's me! The one and only, yours truly! Can I come in?" he asked, removing his big fancy cowboy hat. Reluctantly, she removed the door chain to get a better look at her child's handsome father. She took a few steps backward, speechless. Still hiding her stomach behind the door, she gazed at the man she had been hoping to avoid since that strange night. Taking advantage of the moment, he strutted arrogantly into her apartment. As he rushed by her, the hair on the back of her neck rose on end. She slammed the door, rolling her eyes at his rudeness.

"Ernestine, you look fab—" Stopping, his eyes dropped down to her very pregnant stomach. Thomas's smile shattered, and he was unable to hide the quick flash of disappointment that streaked across his face. Caught off guard, he pointed at her belly.

"You look . . . umm … *preg*nant!"

She stared at him like he was crazy.

"Pooh! Merry Christmas, girl!" He pointed nervously to her stomach again. "La vie est belle! Life *is* beautiful, isn't it?" His voice took on a sardonic tone.

She responded with attitude. "Yeah! Life is *real* pretty! Have a seat, Thomas.

"And pregnant with a child, I might add!"

"Well, Thomas, we did get ourselves pretty wasted that night, if you recall. You know, nine months ago? Ringing any Christmas bells? To see you sitting there is quite the unexpected surprise. And I can't quite put my finger on it, but you look sort of different from the last time I saw you. Hmmm … maybe it's the ridiculous cowboy costume!"

She wanted nothing more than for this happenstance "reunion" to end as soon as possible. To make things more complicated, she started feeling strangely attracted to him. She entertained the idea that his showing up was a possible blessing. After all, he was the child's father. Giving the situation the benefit of doubt, she reconsidered the odd coincidence. *This possibly may very well be a divine act of providence….!*

"So, you aren't married or engaged."

Weary of keeping her secret, a sinister smirk indented her chubby, dimpled face. *The nerve of this arrogant Negro. Let me bust this fool's bubble before it goes any farther!* "No, Thomas, I'm not married. The fact of the matter is I have no fiancée or boyfriend." Pausing, she placed one hand on her stomach and pointed the other at him coldly. "Thomas Delroy, this is your baby. You are the father!" She rubbed her belly, talking to her baby mockingly. "Yeah, it's your daddy, all right!"

It took a minute for it all to soak in. "What do you mean claiming me as the father?" His ego shrank right along with his manhood. He paced the room, sweating nervously and fidgeting with his hat.

"Wow, Ernestine, you know that ain't something to be joking about!" He bent over, looking like he was about to be sick right there on her living room floor. "Wait, wait. I need a minute to think about all this. Hey, I really have to use your bathroom." He placed his hands over his mouth and stomach, dashing past her.

Rubbing her own stomach, feeling nauseated also, she shouted down the hallway after him. "I'm not joking with you about this baby, Thomas, and the bathroom is on the left! Don't you remember?"

Thomas rushed into the bathroom, barely able to lock the door before he got violently sick. "Please, please! This can't be true." Turning on the sink faucets to try to cover up the noise, his body suddenly became abnormally hot, his blood boiling in his veins. He glanced at himself in the mirror. *Why the hell am I dressed like this?* He snatched off the overcoat and tossed it and the cowboy hat on the floor. *Oh, please! I don't even know that woman in there. It was just a drunken one night stand, for Pete's sake! I wish this were not happening to me. I'd give anything to change it all!* Seeing his reflection in the mirror again prompted another bout of retching. Splashing handfuls of the cold water on his face, Thomas stepped back, frightened. Bellowing black clouds filled the interior of the mirror. An old, gray-bearded man in the exact same cowboy get-up stared out from the murk, shaking his head in pity.

"Ooooh, wee boy, you done went and done it now, baby! Bet you got a hell of a surprise thinking on coming back here to dip your stick! You got a heap of trouble with your little girly friend out there! Blessed thee be that I've come to help you outta this mess, partner!" Puffing vigorously on a big cigar, the old cowboy grinned.

"What … what? What the freaking hell are you?" Thomas thought he must be hallucinating.

"I'm your partner, and I said I have come to help you. So listen to what I have to say and stop acting like a damn fool! Think back and remember what happened that night. We stopped by the liquor store for more alcohol and she suggested you buy the condoms. When you went to bed with her, she did that little trick with her mouth and covered you with it. I tell you she is a wicked woman! She cast an evil spell over you that night."

"You say she placed some kind of spell on me?" Entranced, Thomas fell easily for the deception. Ezekiel jumped at the chance to feed him more lies. "Oh, yes! She drew you to the tavern to place her spell on you. It was all a set up to steal your virginity and get your seed to make the baby she now carries in her belly. She laid more than a spell on you that night, partner, as you see."

A light knock on the bathroom door startled them both.

"Are you all right in there, Thomas?" Ernestine asked, worried. Before Thomas could answer, the image jumped from the mirror into his body.

"Yeah . . . yeah, I'm okay. Coming right out!" With glowing eyes, Thomas looked back at the empty mirror as he hurriedly cleaned up his mess. He opened the door and nearly walked right into Ernestine.

"I was just checking to make sure you were all right. I thought I heard you talking to someone. Were you on the phone?"

"No, no. I mean yeah, yeah. The phone. I got a call. You know, that was quite a jolt you gave me."

She suspiciously looked around the clean but smelly bathroom. "Don't tell me you were smoking in my bathroom!" she shouted angrily. Obviously irritated, she pushed him down the hallway and returned to the bathroom. She grabbed a can of disinfectant, giving the room a long spray and complaining loudly. "Oh. My. God. I can't believe you, Thomas!"

"Sorry 'bout that!" Thomas hollered back from the living room. Ezekiel's voice sounded in Thomas' head.

"For all we know, she could have bitten a hole in it just so she *could* get pregnant! You know, that's an old trick!" The laughing evil voice got serious. "Step up, son! Kill the fat bitch and that baby right now and be done with it."

"Are you crazy? I'm not going to kill her! What are you?"

"Okay, then I will!"

Ernestine came back from the bathroom and handed him his coat and hat.

"You look pretty rattled, are you sure you're all right, Thomas? Maybe it would be best if you came back after my trip in the morning so we can talk about things. I know it's a lot to accept all of a sudden."

"You are so right. I need to go clear my head and kind of sort things out! I have to agree, this *is* a lot to deal with." He put on his coat and hat.

"I'll probably be a whole different person by the time you see me again." He smiled. "I'm feeling better about this already."

She watched him walk down the hallway. Waiting for the elevator, he turned and tipped his cowboy hat good-bye and gave a charming salute. She closed the door, smiling. *Maybe this surprise isn't such a bad thing after all.*

Thomas rode the elevator down, jiggling her keys in his coat pocket. "I can't wait to see the look on your face at the surprises you got coming!"

CHAPTER 3

Be Careful What You Pray For

Later that morning, Ernestine realized her house keys were missing. She hustled down to the carport as fast as her condition would allow, fearing the worst. Thomas had stolen her car.

Ernestine screamed at the empty car spot in angry self-pity. "Why would he do something like this to me!? I swear to God I will never have anything to do with you again, Mr. Thomas Delroy."

Ernestine did not hesitate in reporting him to the police. The following hours were shadowed by a dark cloud of gloom. Thomas' unexpected visit, stealing her car, the visit to her parents' tomorrow—uggghhh. She flopped on the bed, confused, out of breath and tired. The more she thought about everything, the more depressed she became. The full impact of telling her parents hit her, causing a large lump to lodge in her throat. *Boy, were they in for an enormous surprise when they see the gift I'm bringing home!* She rubbed her belly as though seeking comfort from her unborn child. Overwhelmed, she got down her knees and began to pray. Feeling a little better, she hauled herself up off the floor and saw her reflection, huge, in the dresser mirror. Picturing her daddy's reaction made her knees quiver. She rubbed her stomach again and released a sad, long-winded sigh. *I would give anything to avoid facing all the drama tomorrow! I should have told Momma about the baby eight months ago. They going to trip. At this point, bring it. I just want to get it over with.* She got ready for bed and crawled beneath her shabby comforter. *Some comfort.* She twirled one of her huge, curly locks around her fingers, not remembering that she used to do the same thing as a child when she couldn't sleep. She finally succumbed, tossing and turning.

* * *

At three forty-five in the morning the skies above Odem erupt with Ezekiel's return, awaking Ernestine. Going over to the window, she looked outside and hollered, elated by the violent, electrical snowstorm raging outside.

"WOO-HOOO! Thank you, Lord, for answering my prayers, thank you, thank you, thank you!"

She could not have asked for a better excuse to cancel her trip to Boston. She returned to bed, ready to spend Christmas snuggled in, curled up and warm. "Thank you again for answering my prayers, Lord! At least they should have received their Christmas card by now." She'd mailed the card off last week, it was her best piece of artwork ever. Wearing a big smile, she giggled, drifting off to thoughts of a worsening storm.

* * *

Christmas Eve morning, the ringing phone woke her up. Answering it, her mother's voice gave her a chill. She stared out the window at the light snow gently falling. She blinked.

"Hello, honey! Merry Christmas! Oh dear, this weather is so unpredictable! We heard about that freak flash storm you had there last night. We have decided we do not want you driving today, so Dad bought a train ticket for you. Isn't he great? The trains are running on schedule this morning. A taxi will pick you up around 9:30, and your train to Boston leaves at ten twenty-eight. All the arrangements are made! Just call us when you get to the train station so we can meet you when you arrive. We can't wait to see you!"

"Me too, Momma! That's great!" She forced a bright manner. "Give daddy my love and Merry Christmas! See you later!" Emotionally deflated, she hung up. She turned on the television to check the weather. The quirky electrical snow was unexplainable. It dumped a lot of snow in a confined area, making travel difficult on city streets, but not impossible. Just as her mother had said, the storm was not nearly as bad as she had thought. Her prayers unanswered, she imagined, for the gazillionth time, the melodramatic scene of her arrival and revealing her nine-months-pregnant-self to her parents for the first time.

Maybe I should just call momma right now and tell them I'm pregnant before I get on that train. Probably best I get all this over with. Yeah, right, who are you kidding? Aww girl, you know they are going to freak out and snap when you show up there, pregnant, without a husband or even a boyfriend!" She let go a loud sigh of surrender, and tried to calm down by wrapping some presents. Tears clouded her eyes as she inspected each name scribed on the label cards for her Christmas gifts to her parents.

"Mookiie and Dat-tee!" She chuckled at her childhood nicknames for them. A lifetime ago.

"Aww, shoot, this is going to be—please excuse what I'm about to say, Lord—one fucked-up Christmas!"

A loud banging sounded at the door. Ernestine's silly first thought was, *God? Great. You've completely lost it.*

"Who's there?"

Instead of a response, the knock came again, the pounding harder. Hoping it was not the taxi arriving early to take her to the train station, she got up from the couch.

"I'm coming, damn it!" Ernestine shouted angrily at the door. "Who is it?"

"Thomas, is that you?" Still no response. The knock banged again. She looked through the peephole, surprised to see no one standing there. Taking a deep breath, she thought about Thomas playing the day before.

"Thomas, is that you?" She repeated, getting agitated. She unlocked the door and swung it open, finding no one in sight. Befuddled, she stepped out into the hall.

"Awww naw, now this is freaking impossible! How could somebody just disappear into thin air like that?" She shouted down the hallway. The cold silence frightened her. As she turned to go back inside, she spied a red envelope taped under the peephole. Looking around, she snatched the envelope off the door and beat a hasty retreat. Locking the door behind her, a sharp chill shot up her spine as she ripped open the bulky envelope. A smaller yellow envelope marked "KEYS" fell out onto the floor. Her heart quickened as she read the accompanying card:

> *If you believe in Christmas*
> *And wishes that come true,*
> *Then there's something special waiting*
> *Outside just for you!*

Assuming the note was from that "missing moron" Thomas, a giant smile slowly spread across her face. "Thank God! He brought my car back!"

She bent over with much difficulty and picked up the small, bulging envelope off the floor, shaking it to heard the keys jingle. Grabbing her coat and her new set of house keys, she rushed out with the envelope clenched in her hands. Not waiting for the slow elevator, she hurriedly took the one flight of stairs down to the lobby. She waddled out of the building into the snow and tried to focus, looking for her Toyota. She stopped dead in her tracks as her eyes widened in disbelief.

"OH. MY. GOD!" she screamed.

Red ribbons blew wildly in the wind, wrapped around a brand new black BMW 750 *LI* parked directly in front of the apartment building. Almost fainting from the sight of it, she had a hard time catching her breath. Flabbergasted and bewildered were not the right words, but they came close. She read the card in her hand again. Shielding her eyes from the wind and snow, she scanned the immediate area. *Where was he?*

She walked up to the magnificent vehicle. Attached to the large, red ribbon was another red envelope, this one huge. The temperature dropped drastically and the wind began to howl like an Alaskan sled team. She anxiously ripped the envelope open, pulling out another unsigned red card. Happy tears filled her eyes. Smiling, she pressed her lips gently against the card. The thoughtful touch of the card written in calligraphy really put her over the edge:

I asked myself, "In His steps, what would Jesus do?"
So here's a brand new gift to the both of you.
I can't wait to see the look on your face
when all your worries are erased.
Merry Christmas!
(I will see you real soon)

She'd obviously thought the keys sealed inside the small envelope were to her old Toyota. Ripping open the top of the envelope, she slid the keys out. She couldn't help herself; she was delighted to see the distinctive BMW logo embedded on the key grips. She pressed down on the unlock button. The car responded immediately with two short, sharp chirps, the sleek lights corresponding, blinking back at her twice. Kissing the keys, she jumped slightly in sheer delight, shouting up to the sky, "YESSSS, Jesus! THANK YOU LORD!" It didn't quite drown out the tiny voice that whispered from her heart, *This isn't exactly what you wished for,* but she still chose to ignore it

A high wind blew her hair into her face as a cab drove up the street. The driver had already decided to add an extra five bucks tip to the prepaid tab.

Ernestine waved the taxi down. He stopped and cracked his passenger window. He hollered to her from behind his gray beard.

"You da lady make for pickup appointment?"

"Oh, if you're here for the nine-thirty pickup to the train station, that's supposed to be for me! I am sorry and thank you for being on time in this weather and all, but I won't be needing your services." She pointed cheerfully to the ribbon- wrapped car.

"It's my unexpected Christmas present!" She shouted joyfully, jingling the keys at the disgruntled taxi man. "And you can keep the fare!" Wearing a huge smile, she gave him a thumbs up and winked.

Finding no humor in her glee, he grumbled obscenities back at her. He flipped a finger at her and a lightning bolt shot across the sky.

She smiled. "You see, God don't like ugly, you know! And a very Merry Christmas to you also, mofo!"

The cab driver pulled away, steaming mad. He took off his ball cap and put on a cowboy hat, transforming into his true self. Ezekiel Joppa looked at her in his rear view mirror. "You're not done with me yet!" he growled.

Ernestine shook her head, watching him drive away, all mad. "My word, the nerve of some people! I wonder why he was so upset, he just got paid for doing nothing. Unbelievable!" She turned to gaze at her new car.

"Now *this* is a wonderful gift, just what I've always wanted. Thank you, Jesus and thank you, Thomas!"

CHAPTER 4

Another Surprise

Ernestine felt great now that a brand new Beemer was sitting pretty in her carport. The phone rang. She wondered which of her parents was calling this time, and now she could not wait to tell them about *everything* that had happened. It was weird how money could make things seem better. She reached for the phone and had another happy thought. *Maybe it was Thomas calling to see if I got the car and make an attempt at straightening things out.*

"Hello?" she answered, full of anticipation.

"Ernestine Jackson, you must leave that apartment now! You are in great danger! Ezekiel has arrived and is coming here for you!" Ernestine didn't recognize the woman's frantic voice. She walked over to the window, listening to her continued warnings.

"You got to get out of there right now or face your death!" the woman cried out to her in dire distress.

"Who is this?" She checked out the empty windy street below. The mysterious voice shouted through the phone.

"Hey! Get out of that window! Leave there *now* you are running out of—"

CLICK. The strange voice was gone.

Frightened, Ernestine shouted into the phone. "Hello ... hello ... is anyone there?"

The receiver filled with the high-frequency sound of an angry swarm of buzzing bees. She covered her ear screaming in pain and slammed the phone down on the hook. A foreign and frightening sense of imminent danger overwhelmed her. The premonition of impending doom had her grabbing her already packed bags and Christmas gifts and fleeing her apartment in terror. She scurried down the hallway, frantically lugging her rolling bag with one arm and balancing gifts in the other, rushing to the elevator. Relieved to see the lobby empty, she rushed out the back exit to the carport. Swirling winds howled around her building.

She fumbled with her keys as she unlocked the car. It tweeted and blinked at her. Freezing wind swished trash and fallen snow down the empty alleyway. She scanned for anything even remotely threating, her senses on high alert. She popped the trunk and all but threw her things in. The howling wind whipped around her body, chilling her to the bone.

"Something evil is out here ... I can feel it!" Her alarming intuition and paranoia were going crazy. The alley safe and clear, she climbed into her car. She'd started it up and was checking the rearview to back out when a ghostly image of an old woman popped up in the back seat. She screamed and reflexively stomped on the brakes, even though the car was not in gear. The apparition fully materialized, oddly dressed in a burgundy Quaker-style bonnet. The ghost looked around, seemingly just as stunned as Ernestine.

"Oh, my God! It's a freaking ghost!" Ernestine shrieked.

"Where?" the woman hollered back in terror. She looked around in fear. Freaking out, both women began screamed at each another until they realized how dreadfully ridiculous they sounded.

"Where am I? How did I get here?" The dazed, distraught ghost asked, out of breath.

"I don't know where you came from, lady. You just appeared out of thin air. Are you some kind of ghost or something?"

The ghost dissipated, reappearing in the passenger seat.

"Oh my God, you just did it again! Will you stop doing that? You are scaring me!" Ernestine wondered if she was losing her own mind.

"*I* am the ghost of which you speak?" She looked at the wavering translucence of her hand. "My goodness! I am!" As though speaking to herself, the ghost said, "It's like one of Jeremiah's dreams…!" Looking at Ernestine, she explained, "My boy would tell me often about dreams he would have of stepping out with a beautiful angel from the future in one of these contraptions." She looked around her in wonderment.

Closely observing the ghost woman, Ernestine realized how well dressed she was, wearing the bonnet together with a tasteful, matching short burgundy cape over her shoulders. The three-buttoned burgundy dress coat, accented by her high-collared, white Victorian blouse made the outfit quite stylish.

"What are you? How did you get here?" Ernestine asked shakily.

The elderly woman looked worried as she addressed the young pregnant girl.

"Please—I will not do you any harm. My name is Mattie, Mattie Stone, and I do not know how I got here. I came to help you—I just know that I must. We must leave here quickly! Ezekiel Joppa is coming, child!"

She received no response.

"You are Ernestine Jackson, are you not?" The old woman, squinting, put on her round rimmed glasses to get a better look at the girl.

Ernestine realized who the woman was.

"It was you on the phone, wasn't it? I do not know what is going on here, but you are scaring the hell out of me! Tell me what you are and how you just appeared in my car!"

A sorrowful look of disappointment dimmed the face of the ghost. "Child, I do not know, as I said! All I know is that I am here to bring you warning and help keep you alive!"

Ernestine glared in shock at the ghost.

"But where do you come from? How do I trust you? I've already had enough strange stuff happen to me this week, and I really can't handle this!"

The apparition took control of the situation. Mimicking Ernestine's voice in the same baby-like manner, the old woman spoke the nicknames of her parents.

"Mookiie, Dat-tee", are the nicknames you called your parents when you were just a baby! Your father . . . your father's name is Girard and your momma ... your momma's name is Dorothy, but everybody calls her Dottie?" She paused. "How could I know that? My, my! I do not know how I know these things myself! What I do know is that this surely is not Mariah, North Carolina in the year 1867."

"What the hell? Did you just say, 1867? North Carolina? Now just wait a damn minute, lady."

"Don't you curse at me, young lady!" The woman held up the cross from the chain around her neck. "I told you I am here to warn and save you and the child from Ezekiel! You have to understand and accept what is going on here child. If we do not leave this place right now we all going to end up dead. Ezekiel is an evil assassin here to kill you and your baby." She pointed up to black clouds forming above the alley in the sky.

"Hell is coming for you! You must trust me! Come on, child, we are out of time. Let's get this contraption going and get out of here! PLEASE!"

Ernestine stared at the woman, confused and speechless.

The ghost slapped her hand against the dashboard as if hitting the backside of a horse. "Giddy this thing up! WE MUST GO! We must get south to Mariah, North Carolina!"

"You must be crazy talking about driving all the way down south just like that!" Ernestine objected.

"Your baby is special and she must be saved." The ghost revealed.

"This is all impossible! I do not believe what you are telling me! That's enough, just get out of my car, please!"

"Trust me, Ernestine, and please, please don't speak like that. If you believe, anything is possible. Nothing is impossible if you have real faith. Have you not, as you said, experienced strange things? Has someone visited you wearing the clothes of a rancher? Someone you know who acted strangely, as though he was not himself?"

Ernestine blanched, frozen, thinking of Thomas' weird visit.

"I thought as much. Ezekiel has already been here. He is going to kill you and take your baby! Please, I beg you, don't put me out!"

"Ok, maybe it is best we start over, from the beginning. What is the last thing you remember before you got here in my car?" The wind began to pick up.

"We really don't have time for this…. The last thing I remember … it is Christmas Eve, 1867. I was in Mariah, standing in front of our store, locking it up with my husband, Seth. We were on our way to meet Jerimiah and the newcomers with that pretty little baby girl at the church christening—then the fog…. The sheriff and his deputies came out of the fog, riding on horseback. The sheriff said he was chasing after the new strangers, they were with my boy. Then the ... then ... then the fireball.... My Lord! Look out! The fire! Seth, the fireball!" Covering her face, she slowly dropped her hand and looked around. "The next thing I know, I am here with you in this contraption. I do know one thing, we have to leave here now and join the others in the South to prepare for the real battle that is coming! We done wasted too much time already!" The alley grew darker and the wind blew. "And you can forget about getting any help from that baby's daddy! You were under an evil spell the night of your conception. Thomas is not the same person that you hope he is, thank you very much! He serves the Moloch! Now let us leave this place!"

Questions explode like a firework finale in Ernestine's mind. *How could Thomas have something to do with this? People appearing out of nowhere ... claiming to be from 1867 ... an evil assassin sent here to kill my child and me. Am I to believe all this or am I going crazy? And what the hell is a Moloch?*

The howling wind suddenly stopped, and everything became eerily silent and still. A dense fog bank rolled in at both ends of the alley. The child inside Ernestine's stomach kicked violently, as if in distress. Her paranoia rising, Ernestine's legs began to shake.

Mattie screamed out, pointing down to the opposite end of the alley at the fog.

"Look! He has come! It's him ... he's here!"

Ernestine, dizzy and sick to her stomach, watched as the sudden spinning fog barreled down the alley toward them.

"What's happening? What is going on?" She shouted over to the petrified Mattie, who vanished.

"Hey, come back here, you are supposed to help me!" Ernestine hollered. Mattie reappeared outside the car. Ernestine opened the window, but before she can get a word out, the woman hollered desperately, "Get out of here, he's here! Save that child!"

Ernestine unlocked the car doors, leaned over and opened the passenger door.

"Get in here, come on! We're going to the police!"

The woman refused, shaking her head in response.

"It is too late for that! This is something the law cannot do anything to stop! I do not belong here in this time or place! We are worlds apart! May the Lord be with you!" The car door closed and locked under its own power.

The ghostwoman stepped away from the car and walked down the middle of the alley, frantically screaming through the open window and waving Ernestine off.

"Believe what I have told you! Ride south to North Carolina to a town called Mariah. Find the church there ... and seek sanctuary from the Reverend Bishop. Save the baby, the child is what Joppa has come to—"

Before she could finish, the car stereo began blasting James Brown. A black pick up with roaring flames painted on the front hood cannonballed out of the fog, blasting the song, "The Big Payback." The truck slammed into

Mattie, shattering her body into a thousand pieces of glass crystal.

The black Chevy skidded to a stop and abruptly rose off the ground. It spun in mid-air and peeled toward the beemer.

"Help me, Jesus!" Ernestine screamed. Reacting out of sheer terror, she slapped the gearshift into reverse, stomping down on the gas pedal. The high-performance BMW responded immediately. It took off, whipping out of the carport backward, speeding blindly down the foggy alley in reverse.

The pickup missed ramming into her car by inches. Ezekiel Joppa grinned. As the headlights of the fleeing BMW disappeared into the fog, he gunned the engine after her.

The BMW shot out of the alley like a bullet into the street. Miraculously, there was no fog there and she barely missed driving straight into traffic! She skidded to a stop across the street in the opposite alley. The black Chevy leapt out of the foggy alley in hot pursuit and pounced right into the middle of the busy intersection. Seeing Ernestine's car speeding backward down the alley across the street, the paranormal nightmare of a man growled in anger and frustration like a starved wolf losing his prey. He made to gun the engine again when a siren-blasting fire truck broadsided his truck. The powerful impact popped out the front windshield and the pickup tumbled down the street in flames. It flipped over, crashing into parked cars and burning ferociously out of control.

At the moment of impact, the music inside Ernestine's car abruptly shut off. She drove slowly out to the street to get a better look.

Firefighters scrambled to extinguish the fire, trying to save the burning man trapped inside. She pulled up closer. He screamed, burning alive, trapped, still strapped in his seatbelt and hanging upside down, his cowboy hat burning in flames. They all stood witness as he stopped his wails of anguish. As she passed, she glimpsed the face. It's the same as the bearded cabbie that was going to take her to the train station earlier.

"I'm not done with you, yet. I'll see you again!" he shouted, flipping her off. He grinned, pretending to shoot her in the face, and his body became fully consumed in flames. To everyone's amazement, the burning truck transformed into a swirling ball of fire. Mystically, the man and truck instantly disappeared into thin air. Astonished, the frightened firemen back away. Not knowing what was going to happen next, many of those gathered began to stampede away from the scene.

Well, that all was more than too much for Ernestine. She peeled off and turned the corner onto her street. She stopped in time to see her apartment explode in flames. The fire engine had been en route to put out the fire at her burning building.

"Awww, hell naw!" Ernestine hollered out in horror. She prayed for her apartment neighbors, hoping they got out in time. She sped off in tears.

The BMW raced onto the ramp of Interstate 95, heading south. Some force was mystically guiding her south. Ernestine pulled to the side of the road and stared blankly at the confusing freeway signs. Running for her life and not really understanding why, Ernestine desperately searched for reasons and answers. A dark storm brewed on the horizon ahead of her.

"What am I doing? Where am I going? What is the purpose behind all this? Was the ghost actually a divine Spirit of some kind sent here as a messenger?"

Her parents came to mind again. Ernestine recited her favorite poem aloud. Her father had written and given it to her before she left for college.

"He Is Always There"
There will come a time when you can't go home
And there will be a time when you will feel alone.
There will come times when you cannot go back
And you may face a time you live to regret.
However, there is one blessed fact
that you should never forget.
There will never come a time when
God does not love you.
There will never be a time when
God will not forgive you.
There will never come a time when God does not care
And there will never be a time
when God is not there!

A whisper spoke softly into her ear. "*Marrriah!*" Her face lit up. "Woooo hooo, Mariah! That's it! Praise the Lord, Mariah … Mariah . . . North Carolina … that's the name of the town!" Exuberant, she tries hard to remember the names of the men the ghost had spoken to her. Her radio blasted on again, playing that James Brown song. The music got louder and the flaming hood of the black Chevy pickup appeared, slowly pulling up alongside her, flying above the ground, in perfect condition. Ezekiel Joppa smiled pleasantly over at her. Slowly, she forced herself to look up into the cab. Tipping his big black cowboy hat, he flipped that finger at her again. It flamed up, and he lit a cigar sticking out the corner of his mouth. He gave her a wave. She screamed.

"Oh, my God, no ... no, it can't be you!" He rammed the pick up into the side of her car. The attempt to spin her off the road backfired as his truck spun off instead. Out of control, the black truck crashed into a large tree.

The weird music immediately stopped playing in her car. The 750 *LI* sped down the slippery roadway, disappearing into the thick fog. She flipped a finger and a victory sign into the dark rearview mirror. "Yeah baby, woo hooo! Now that's what I'm talking abooout! I love this car!" Her joyous celebration was short lived. Sharp pains ripped from her womb up her right side. She grabbed and unharnessed her seat belt to ease the pain and pressure.

Ezekiel, driving his smashed-up Chevy, rammed violently into the rear end of her car. He succeeded this time in sending her BMW spinning dangerously out of control.

"Aaaaaaaggghhh! MMmoooookeeiiie!" she screamed, pulling frantically on the door handle. Her car careened off the road, crashing into a large oak tree and bursting into flames. A swirling cloud of grey fog encased the black pick up, raising it off the ground. The cloud burst into a flaming burning orb, disappearing with James Brown's screaming voice fading into the silent cold night. It began to storm.

Several miles down the road from the Ernestine's accident, a road sign read:

Welcome to "God's Country"
Mariah, North Carolina
Established 1867 Population 367

Meanwhile, at the home of Ernestine's parents in Boston, Dorothy was busy getting ready, waiting anxiously to hear from her daughter. Overwhelmed by a bad feeling, she began to worry.

Why haven't I heard from her?

CHAPTER 5

The Quest

Cold, cloudy skies greeted the winter's morning in Mariah. The delicious aromatic blend of hazelnut cinnamon coffee wafted through John Davidson's warm house. He sat watching the early morning news in his big recliner, sipping on his fresh brew. Walking into the bathroom, he turned on the shower and disrobed. He took a moment to look at his naked body in the full-length mirror. He admired himself, flexing his buff, chocolate-brown muscles in competition-style poses until the hot steam filled the mirror and covered his vanity. He jumped into the shower, jumping right back out, screaming in agony, scalded by the piercing-hot water. After adjusting the temperature, he finished a long, relaxing shower. Wetting his face to shave, he remembered the can of shaving cream he left in the bag on the kitchen counter from shopping last night. Naked, with his towel hanging from his neck, he stepped out of the bathroom. Walking down the hallway, the sweet scent of lilac and lilies had replaced the strong coffee aroma.

A woman sat in his recliner intensely watching television; she was not aware of John's approach. He entered the living room, stopping dead in his tracks, startled by the uninvited visitor.

"Faith Matthews, what are you doing showing up in my house like this unannounced? That's not cool."

She sprung up, jumping out of the chair with the prowess and agility of a startled cat.

John noticed that she was oddly dressed in a black monk's robe as she defensively grabbed hold of the handle of a sword strapped to her side.

Naked and confused, John stepped back. "Hey, hold on, why are you dressed like that Faith? And what in Sam Hill are you carrying a sword around for? What's going on with you?"

Not attempting to cover his body, a sly, shrewd smile spread across his face as he walked toward her. "How did you get in here?"

Seeing him approach in all his glory, she closed her eyes, raising her arms to stop him.

"No, John. Stop right there, please, I must explain. You don't understand, I'm not who you think I am. It's Hope. Hope Matthews!"

"Uhhhh…. Why are you calling yourself Hope?"

She covered her face with her hands. "It truly is me. I am Hope, John, and please, you need to go put something on!"

John covered himself with his towel. "That's impossible, and not very funny at all, Faith! Playing around like that about your sister is so disrespectful! How dare you joke in such a way! You know Hope is dead, Faith! How can you even make such a cruel and mean joke? That's very sick, you know!"

Still covering her closed eyes, Hope attempted to explain. "I know this may seem impossible to you . . . but it is me, it is truly me, I am Hope, John! I have returned to Mariah to partake in a quest we must face together, John. Almost like when we were last together." Hope peeped to see that John had covered himself and slowly dropped her hands, revealing her naturally beautiful, angelic face.

"Now, I beg of you, please go and put some clothes on. We must talk!"

John, stumped by this explanation, questioned whether his fiancée had gone and lost her mind. John stared, speechless, enchanted by her smiling hazel brown eyes. Her brown skin glowed. Simply put, like her twin sister, Faith, she had the face of an angel.

Hope began to explain. "We are…"

"All clear in the back, here," a voice interrupted.

Seeing the armed, hooded intruder enter with sword drawn, John held his hands up, preparing to defend himself. His towel dropped to the floor. The intruder pushed her hood back. John was shocked to see it was the ex-sheriff, Angela Solomon. Awkwardly standing stark naked in front of two women, their eyes automatically dropped to John's midsection with raised eyebrows. In shock, John froze, standing there buck naked with his mouth hanging open.

This was incredible. The last time he saw her she had died along with Hope! He stared at her hair, which she parted Indian-style down the middle. She was wearing two long, thick braids, one on each side of her face, extending past her shoulders. They were striking. The one on the right was a bright red, and the other royal blue. She looked serene and majestic.

Angela frowned disapprovingly at his stare. Embarrassed, he covered himself with both hands and snatched the towel up off the floor. She pulled her hood back over her head and swiftly turned away in disgust as she sheathed her weapon. Hope smirked while she halfheartedly shielded her eyes.

"This is impossible, seeing you both here together! How can this be?" he stated, completely baffled, securing the towel tightly around his waist.

The silent awkward moment turned very uncomfortable.

Angela's hands gripped tightly the two golden swords at her side. Marching across the room to the front door, she instructed John, "Please just do as Hope asked and put on some clothes! You must prepare. We must hurry, there is danger here."

She pressed her ear against the door to avoid looking at John. She listened intently for movement outside.

"Brought anybody else back from the grave with you?" John cynically asked.

"No. We are the only ones, so far. Hurry. I have a lot to explain and we do not have time to waste," Hope responded, sounding anxious.

"Oh, o*kay*, give me a minute to get dressed." Perplexed, John retreated down the hallway toward his bedroom. The two women frowned when he stopped midway, turned and rushed back into the kitchen.

"Ummmmm, my apologies about the towel and all, I was in the middle of my shower . . . I mean shave, I was coming in here to get the shaving cream." He gestured clumsily causing his towel to slip again.

"John, please … just get dressed! Do what you have to do—we have to get started!" Hope's command was halfhearted. She hadn't thought it would affect her so deeply to see him again in the—so to speak—flesh.

"Yes . . . yes, of course, you're right, Faith. . . . Wow! Sorry, I mean Hope! I'll be right out!"

Worry covered her face. Concerned, she got up and joined Angela in checking the windows, scanning the woods outside.

John grabbed the shaving cream from the counter, trying hard to hide a big, silly grin on his face. He scurried back into the bathroom, filled with excitement. He stared, mesmerized, into the mirror, reflecting on the day he'd last seen the two women alive. *This seems impossible. I can hardly believe Hope and Sheriff Solomon are sitting in my living room right at this moment, still alive! How can it be? What the hell was this all about?*

In apprehensive silence, the two women sat silently as they waited for John to finish dressing. They watched the news coverage of the unnatural electrical snowstorm anomaly that had occurred during the night. The news brought confirmation. Ezekiel Joppa had already arrived, for only he could conjure up such a strange phenomenon. Angela was first to comment.

"The Moloch that returns here has gained much strength. Much has changed in the short time since we left!"

Hope silently nodded her head in agreement. "Yes, there is much that has changed since our departure. That is why we have return to Mariah, isn't it? To make things right?" Her eyes filled with tears.

John, meanwhile, rushed to finish his shave. He dashed into the bedroom, opening the closet. The same type of robe the women had on hung on the back of the door. Removing it, hooked underneath, he found a golden double-edged sword. "What the…?" John reached under the bed. Proudly, he pulled out a box. Inside was new pair of Nike Air Jordans. The new-edition high top white leather two-hundred-dollar basketball shoe had hit the stores just in time for Christmas. It took him over ten minutes to double lace the new high top shoes, using red and white shoestrings. Fully shod, he dressed in the black robe. It fell all the way to the floor, covering his new Nikes. John looked at himself with a broad smile. "Perfect!" Prepared, John swaggered into the living room. His heart and mind filled with memories of the love he once held for the twin sister of his fiancée. It was hard to believe they were there, but he now knew the reason.

"The Moloch has returned," John knowingly stated.

Hope spoke first.

"Yes, John. Their leader, Ezekiel himself, is here gathering many to serve him. I know you have many questions. For now, as we told you, our return is because of him. We have a quest to fulfill to save and protect a woman and her unborn child. At this moment, Ezekiel desperately seeks to capture the child's mother and make a sacrifice of them both. We will have plenty of time to talk more as we journey together on this quest. Be wary and understand deceptions and challenges to make us weak are already set into motion to try to defeat our purpose," she warned.

"I understand completely!" John stated. "So let's go get Faith and begin our quest!"

"Faith will not be joining us. She has to stand her ground here in Mariah and face and defeat challenges of her own while we journey, John."

"Oh … so then it's just going be the sheriff, you and me traveling together?"

"It will be just the three of us for now, others will join our cause later," Hope replied.

Her ambiguous answer and Faith not joining them confused John. There was a long pause before he spoke.

"Will she be one of the others joining us later?"

"I don't know the answer to that question, John."

"Why don't we call and tell her and your mom you are here?"

"No, John, they must not know that I am here. They will come to know all in time and on time." Hope insisted, "All will come to light in time and on time."

"Oh, I see…. Well, since that's the way things are let's get on with our quest and save the pregnant damsel in distress. I am ready to bust me up some Moloch, anyway!"

Angela turned away from the door, infuriated. His immature mockery was not funny to the ex-sheriff. Her grip tightened around the handles of both swords. She spoke harshly to them both.

"Listen to me, John, you need to check yourself, this is not a time for foolishness! Our quest is nothing to take lightly or joke about! The child and the mother are in great danger as we speak and here we are wasting time! I pray that we are not too late already! The Moloch threaten everything should they succeed this time. Does that make for any type of humor to you?"

"Whoa, whoa, wait a minute, Sheriff Serious!" John sniped back rudely, holding up a pausing hand. "I was just joking! I realize the importance of this! What is it, Angela, have you lost your sense of humor since you left?"

The two glared scornfully at each other in heated silence.

Hope was disappointed. John had definitely changed. She wondered what had happened to him since she'd gone. His lack of respect and snippy little attitude toward the sheriff was so not like him.

Noticing Hope's look of disappointment, John quickly changed his attitude.

"My bad, I hear you, Sheriff. You are so right! Please forgive me! I understand the importance of all this. I'm thankful that I have been chosen to join in the quest. I'm more than ready to go kick some aaa . . . eh hum I mean. . .

go save the mother and child!" John picked up the remote, turning off the TV. He walked over and swung open the door, bowing. "Ladies first!" Hope walked past and John's eyes filled with lust, reflecting on his naked encounter with her. He turned his head to find the sheriff standing next to him, frowning. She slowly walked by, rolling her eyes and giving him a loathing look of disgust. Outside, Angela gave Hope a grave look of concern as John locked up his place.

"Our time here is not long, but our journey will be. I cannot allow your emotions to interfere or compromise this in any way. I warn you. John must face his challenges soon."

Hope said nothing. Angela took point, leading them through the woods, following the brisk, howling wind. Hope and John walked together in uncomfortable silence.

John spoke first.

"It is hard to believe you are here walking next to me, Hope! The sheriff, too.... Both . . . both of you came back?" He asked, barely able to contain his composure.

Hope reluctantly nodded her head, noting his heightened anxiety. He felt strange saying her name. He desired to touch her to make sure she was real and took hold of her hand.

"I've really missed you, Hope!"

Seeing him expressing a loving look of affection, she snatched her hand away. Hope found herself suddenly getting angry being touched by him. It took all she had to hide the confusion she was experiencing. A tad woozy,

Hope looked over to see Angela closely scrutinizing them both.

Angela pulled her sword from its sheath, shouting to Hope and John.

"The mother and child are in grave danger! Come on, follow me." Angela took off running.

Heeding her command, they raced through the woods as a bitter coldness took over. Delayed rumbling echoes of thunder followed faint flashes of lightning dancing in the distant black clouds approaching from the west. Their desperate search led them to the outskirts of Mariah.

"Fan out! Those we seek are nearby," Angela ordered, as a faint smell consisting of sulfur, burning gasoline, wood and metal floated by. The scent led to a large oak tree, where she found Ernestine Jackson's BMW still smoldering from the accident. Checking inside, there were no occupants. Searching further in the surrounding area, she came across a woman 's body.

"Hey, over here, hurry up! I've found her. Hope, John, she's over here!"

Ernestine Jackson lay on her back. A look of contentment rested on her pretty face; her dead eyes were open in a stare of pleasant wonderment. Wearing a leather coat, her arms crossed over her chest, protecting something. Gently closing her eyes and moving the young woman's arms to her sides, Angela carefully opened the coat to discover the baby lying with her head resting upon her mother's chest.

They looked at peace, motionless, as if they were sleeping. The umbilical cord was still attached, and

Angela she cut it with her sword. Kissing the mother gently on the forehead, tears began to fall down Angela cheeks as she picked up the stillborn child.

John was the first to reach her, and he stared in shock at seeing Ernestine's lifeless body.

"Are we too late, have we failed before our quest has even begun?" he asked, questioning their mission.

"I think they are both dead?" Angela said. "Give me your robe, John!" she commanded.

Quickly removing his robe, John stared oddly at the face of the dead woman as Angela covered the child's body.

"You look as though you know her, John?" she asked.

"She does look familiar, but I can't place from where. Do you think she was from Mariah?"

"Doubt it." Angela looked at him with a peculiar sadness.

Hope ran out from the woods. Her face crumpled seeing the others gathered over the body.

"Lord! No, no, no!" she screamed, running over to them.

Wrapped in John's robe, Angela handed the lifeless child over to an anguished Hope, who cuddled the newborn in her arms and uncovered the child's face. "We have failed in our quest before it's even begun. We have arrived too late to save and protect the mother and the child from evil's harm and I know not what to do." Weeping in sorrow, she cradled the female child, looking at her beautiful, lifeless face. Hope's tears fell on the child's forehead. A rumble of thunder rolled overhead.

John and Angela watched as the baby's body began to glow a bright, pale blue. They stood witness as the child took a deep breath and moved ever so slightly. She burst out with a loud, healthy cry.

Hope smiled, proclaiming with joy, "Look, she is alive, John!"

"She is alive!" Angela cried. "Thanks be to God!"

When Hope tried to hand the baby over to John, the child started screaming and crying in distress. John backed away, intimidated by the child's adverse reaction "No, no I can't! I mean ... she is too fragile! Sh- she ... I'm not used to being around babies ... I don't want to drop her or something!" He turned away.

Hope handed the baby to Angela, overjoyed the child was alive. The crying stopped as soon as they touched. Angela immediately fell in love with the child.

John nervously asked, "You said we were to save and protect both mother and child?"

"I can't answer that question, John. All I know was that now we have to protect this child at all costs." In a low voice, Angela cautioned, "These woods have ears. We should not even speak of her existence in this desecrated spot."

Overhead, the skies darkened. The sound of howling wolves hidden in the woods caused everyone to pause.

"I fear it may have already gotten back to the Moloch that the child lives!" Again, the baby began to cry out of control. A thick black mist appeared and began swirling around them.

Angela shouted. "The Moloch are here! They have found us!"

Pairs of large, gray cat-eyes appeared by the hundreds in the dark, swirling fog. She sets the child at her feet, drawing both her swords.

"Come on, Moloch! Come and taste my blades, evil ones!" Angela shouted.

The Moloch demons launched their attack. Striking swords collided, causing flashing bolts of blinding lightning to strike out. The three suddenly vanished, taking the child with them.

Their attackers stood in the spot where the four were just seconds before, dazed and bewildered. Their angry, beastly commander pushed through.

"Out of my way you fools!" Ezekiel stooped and grabbed a handful of dirt, holding it up to his crooked nose.

"Mmmmm…." He purred, licking the palm of his hand. "Ha, ha, ohoo yeessss! I can still taste the pureness of the child!"

The Chevy pick-up emerged from the thick mist and pulled up next to him. The door opened and the flames painted on the hood ignite in real fire. He lit his cigar on the blazing hood. His horde waited at attention for orders.

The old cowboy spit and jumped, in the flaming truck yelling, "You dudes were worthless. I need a new posse!" He flipped a finger at the stupefied soldiers. "It begins, so let's get this party started. Hallelujah!" he exclaimed, laughing ecstatically. The truck exploded into a fireball and disappeared into the fog.

CHAPTER 6

A Dream Come True

The three materialized in the woods, disoriented, swinging and slashing their swords blindly in the fog surrounding them until they realized they were alone. They all were relieved to find the bundled-up robe was with them still on the ground. Angela picked up the baby and lifted the robe to look at her. The child was safe, resting peacefully. Amazingly, however, the newborn had grown to the size of a six-month-old child during their little disappearing act mere seconds before. The child smiled up at her. She smiled back, kissing the child tenderly. Angela mentioned nothing of this occurrence to the others.

The strange, white blanket of fog hid the winter's sunrise. They realized that they were standing in the middle of a trail. Cautiously, the three walked down the trail in hunt of their gray-eyed attackers. Eventually, they concluded that they had traveled out of harm's way. They could not see a yard in front of them as they slowly walked along the fog-laden trail.

Angela spoke. "We are safe here for now! Come, we need to seek shelter."

For John it felt like hours had passed as they ventured further into the woods. He tried to make out the countryside from what he could see through the thick fog. The well-traveled path seemed all-too-familiar to him. The dried winter foliage crunched loudly under his Nikes, announcing their presence. Meanwhile, the two women walked on the dried leaves making no sound at all.

Somehow, John was dressed in yet another black monk's robe. The child slept warmly, cuddled up in his old one.

"Follow me," Angela beckoned, holding the child cradled in one arm, her drawn sword in the other.

The woods came alive as small animals and winter birds scurried about following the trio and child. A solemn old gray owl also followed, lurking behind in the shadows.

"What shall we call her?" Hope asked.

"We should name her Easter, as she was brought to life by the tears of Hope." Angela wisely answered.

Hope agreed. "She is a very special child."

John stopped them and furrowed his brow. "So where are we?"

They said nothing and walked by him.

"Well.... This is still Mariah, isn't it?" He asked in distress as they passed. The two women continued walking, disappearing into the fog, leaving John standing alone, pondering this quandary. "Aww, come on, you guys!

Will somebody tell me what's going on?" he shouted, getting irritated.

"Not now, John, not now! You will understand soon enough," Angela shouted back.

He caught up with them. "Hey, I'm getting a little tired of this later for the information stuff, so what's up?" The wind shifted in their direction and the air filled with a symphony of the wonderful smells of hickory smoked meats and cooking food. John's attention and mood suddenly changed as he smelled the fragrant aroma of meats, chicken and wild turkey, roasting. Taking a deep breath, the tantalizing unmistakable aroma of barbeque filled his nostrils! They were back in the woods of Mariah; he was sure of that now. He turned to Hope.

"Who else cooked like that outside in the wintertime except good old Mr. Collins? Don't you remember Mr. Collins, Hope? He's getting his fried turkey and famous St. Louis baby back rib dinners ready to sell for Christmas!" His mouth watered and both heard John's stomach grumble.

"Yes, I do!" Hope remembered, smiling. She placed her hand on John's arm firmly so she could explain what was really going on. Taking her by surprise, John jerked out of her grasp. As quick as a jackrabbit, John snatched his robe above his knees and zipped off, disappearing into the fog.

"That's Mr. Collin's cooking I smell I'm telling you!" he shouted back, on the run, full of excitement.

"Wait! John! This is not the same Mariah we just left! Did you hear me, John? It's not the same Mariah!" Hope hollered into the murk. Long moments of silence passed.

"What do you mean this isn't the same Mariah we just left, Hope?" John stopped dead in his tracks. His voice came out of the fog with a notable tone of disgruntlement attached. Before Hope could answer, they heard the screech of a large bird and the fog began to swirl as before.

Tree branches broke and brush crushed beneath the feet of a huge beast charging up the path. The ground pounded beneath them from the thing stampeding on the narrow path, still hidden in the fog. It was heading straight toward the women and child. Hope yelled out in panic.

"John, get back here! Something's coming!" Before her plea could echo through the fog, John was returning down the path toward her, his sword drawn.

"I'm coming, Hope!" he yelled. The women stood at the ready, weapons drawn, and faced the approaching sound.

Whatever the unseen threat was, it was huge and closing in fast on the two women and the child. A huge black beast leapt from the fog.

"Watch out, Hope!" Not a second too soon, John jumped from the fog, pushing her out of harm's way. In the process, he knocked Angela and the baby down directly into the path of the galloping beast. Shrieking a terrorizing neigh, the huge black steed reared up on its hind legs. The wild horse's stomping hooves pounced violently around Angela and the child lying on the ground, trapped underneath. Angela desperately moved about, miraculously dodging the deadly hooves. Clouds of steam bellowed from flared nostrils; the huge black horse kicked wildly into the freezing air. Clinging tightly to the baby and her sword, Angela rolled to safety from underneath the horse.

A flowing red streak caught Angela's eye for a split second. She stood up from the near-death experience in time to see the back side of the dark-clad rider and his horse galloping off. The ends of the red scarf covering his face flowed in the air behind him and were the last to fade into the fog.

"Come back and face me, you coward!" she shouted at the man in anger.

The heavy voice of the man riding the horse bounced back through the fog.

"Whoa ... Whoa ... Maribel!" The horse reacted to her master's command and strong grip on the reins.

Hope yells out to Angela, "Are you all right?"

"We are fine!"

The man glanced back, unable to see the troupe through the thick fog. The red scarf that covered his face whipped in the howling wind. Angela and the baby in her arms were safe and unscathed. John looked amazed at his sword as it returned to its original form, the Altar Cross.

Hearing the horse's slow approach through the fog, they took up defensive positions. The masked man emerged from the opaque fog like a giant black ghost. He wore a big, black wide-brim Stetson cowboy hat pulled down eyebrow-low and cocked to the side. A thick, bright-red wool scarf pulled up over the bridge of his nose left only a tight slit of an opening for his eyes. His long, heavy black overcoat gave him the appearance of a notorious highwayman of some sort.

His eyes bucked with surprise looking over at Angela's beautiful, angry face. Shocked from the sight of her, he whispered to his horse Maribel in bewilderment. "Well, I'll be.... Tis my angel, Maribel ... she has returned just as she promised!"

The big man quickly dismounted. His coat and scarf flowed with the wind as he walked straight toward Angela and the child.

Angela stood, fuming, staring angrily at the approaching dark-clad man. "Hold your ground, mister! Make no sudden moves or I will run my blade right through you."

He stopped immediately and could not help admiring the blade of gold Angela was pointing at him. He looked with curiosity at Angela's odd red and blue braids. As if standing in front of royalty he smoothly removed his hat unveiling a full afro of woolly hair. Respectfully he places his hat over his heart and bows. With much charisma, he spoke to her.

"My Jesus, before my very eyes my dreams have come true and she stands right here! Is it truly you, my angel? You promised you would return to me and here you are and this is no dream!" He extended his other hand in a friendly gesture.

Flabbergasted by his statement and his strangely familiar voice, she pressed her golden sword firmly against his chest and backed him up. His crazy remarks and the act he was putting on as if he knew her confounded her.

Angela's suspicions rose more so when the man did not attempt to remove the red scarf covering his face.

"Raise your hands and place them on the back of your head and I warn you, don't try anything foolish, sir!" She spoke in a strong police tone, pushing her blade against his chest. Hat in hand, he obeyed her orders. Angela placed her sword under his chin. Even in the fog, the blade of gold shone. She wore another golden sword sheathed on her left side. Never had he seen such magnificent weapons. He wondered why these travelers dressed as religious monks carried such precious weapons.

"My angel ... it is me, my love … Jeremiah . . . Jeremiah Stone, and I surely would do you no harm, my lady."

Though flattered, it troubled her, this masked stranger speaking to her as if he knew her. His next statement floored her.

"My angel, we have met before! Do you not remember? You are my guardian angel. We fought side by side during the war against the confederates right here in the battle of Mariah. You saved my life. You are my dream come true!"

Being from the future, Angela had no idea what he was talking about and decided it was time to see who the man with the familiar voice that hid behind the red scarf really was.

"Then you should have no qualms about revealing yourself! Hold steady, sir!" she warned. Pressing her blade firmly against his chin with the tip of her sword, she slipped off the red scarf. Uncovering his handsome dark face, Angela gasped in amazement and covered her mouth with her sword hand. *Oh my God, I do know this man!* She looked comical with her weapon in her hand, the sword point straight up in the air. She stood motionless in silent disbelief.

However, it was his next statement that surprised them all.

"I have been waiting for your return to Mariah. Alas, you have come back as promised and this time in the flesh, not in my dreams! What kind of magic is this, or should I say, more appropriately, what miracle do I witness that you stand here before me, my angel?"

Angela wondered, *Can this truly be That Guy? Can it truly be him?* His mention of a dream come true is exactly what he was to her! They'd met the week before she died, one hundred and fifty years into the future!

He'd appeared every night in her dreams that week! She fell in love with her fairytale dream man, to whom she gave the adorable nickname That Guy, but how could it possibly be the same dream man from her future?" Still dazed and astounded, Angela backed away.

Alarmed by Angela's strange reactions, the big hunk of a man immediately apologized. "I did not mean to startle or frighten you, my dear, but a big old grey owl back there flew right into Maribel's face and spooked her. I would never have been able to forgive myself had we harmed you or your baby! It's a miracle that I did not!"

His utterly charming smile made her heart race and her knees weak. Yet to utter a single word to the man of her dreams was impossible. She found herself staring, confused and speechless, mesmerized by That Guy.

C H A P T E R   7

That Perfect Date

J eremiah Stone stood six feet five inches tall, his muscular body buff like a lumberjack. A twenty-six-year-old, respected Civil War veteran he was by many standards quite the handsome rough-looking black man. He captivated Angela with episodes of the extraordinary dreams he had of his romantic pursuit of her. While they traveled, his three new friends found themselves most fascinated by his story about the day his beloved angel saved his life at the battle that took place in Mariah.

"I held the rank of Private First Class, with 'B' company of the 55th Massachusetts Volunteer Infantry Regiment of the Union Army. We were the second only all-Negro brigade that saw action during the war.

"It was in the summer of '65 during the deadly battle here when God sent a beautiful guardian angel to stand and fight beside me. She stood like a human shield protecting me from all the deathly mayhem that shot and exploded around me that day! We fought together side by side in hand-to-hand combat against them Gray Jackets. I tell you one thing, all those Confederate soldiers that fell before her blades got the chance to see her glory before taking their last breath and meeting their maker!

"Of the whole regiment, only twenty-two of us survived this battle before reinforcements took over the town and the victory. The loss of most of my brothers in arms during those dark hours of battle in these foggy woods still haunts me! After the war, I got my calling to stay here. I voluntarily took on the job of caretaker of the cemetery to wait on the return of my angel, as she promised.

"My uncle and aunt, Seth and Mattie Stone, received their calling to come soon after and moved here to Mariah, opening the general store. I swear as I stand before you an angel came to me that day and fought side by side with me. After the battle, she promised me that she would return to Mariah and the honest to God's truth is she looked just like you!" He finished solemnly, confused. His mind still fought over whether Angela was his battle angel. For both, crossing paths today was truly a dream come true.

Jeremiah led the group toward the clearing where the construction of the Church of God was under way. A large smile spread across his face as he turned and asked, "Are you *sure* you are not the angel that saved me that day, my lovely?"

"I'm so sorry to say again, I'm sure, Jeremiah, it is quite impossible I am that angel!" She smiled sadly.

"We know God can work in mysterious ways! My aunt says with enough faith nothing is impossible. My Aunt Mattie was born a free Negro and graduated college, and she loves to listen to my dream dates with my angel. She says they remind her of the fairytales she used to love to read in school," Jeremiah bragged to Angela.

"My Uncle Seth had a hard time with my stories about you—oh, sorry—I mean my angel. He told me I should stop dreaming and get me a real-life wife of my own!" He grinned, looking at her affectionately. "But my aunt loves to hear about my dream encounters that always start in a big city faraway somewhere in the future … in a different kind of America."

His mention of dream meetings sparked her interest.

"I would like to hear one of these dreams of yours, Jeremiah," Angela requested fondly.

"It would be my pleasure!" He smiled and began to tell them of his favorite dream…

He sits in their kitchen having an early morning breakfast, entertaining his aunt.

"Mattie, I had me one of them dreams last night and boy was it a good one!"

"I can't wait to hear it!" Mattie replies, getting comfortable moving to her rocker. Jeremiah prances around, telling his story that takes place in the future.

"We both were dressed sharper than a knife and the most handsomous couple out to paint the town red!" He pretends to be walking arm in arm with his gorgeous date getting into an automobile. "We would drive around the city in a fancy metal carriage driven without horses."

Mattie questions this. "No horses, you say? Then how do they get around?"

Jeremiah goes through the motions of entering a car and sitting behind the steering wheel. He begins to exaggerate a little. "I even drove one myself!"

Engrossed, she watches him explain systematically driving the horseless buggy.

"You stick a key in it and press your foot on a pedal sticking out the floor and give it what they call some gas, Auntie! You hold on to the steering wheel and off it goes. When you want to stop, you put your foot on the brake just like a horse drawn wagon! It's easy." He begins acting cool, grinning and waving out the window at imaginary people, pretending he is driving around town.

"They are some of the most magical fastest fantastic beautiful things on four wheels you could ever imagine. We traveled on hard black top roads covered with tar. The streets filled with all kinds of other horseless carriages roaming about out in all directions through the city and boy, were they fast! The cities, all the people driving around in horseless carriages, everything is different way in the future."

Mattie's eyes fill wide with imagination. "My, oh my!" Mattie rocks in her chair as she listens intently.

"The city night was all lit up outside by magical lights so bright it was like it was day time. Towering buildings like the ones you talk about in New York City, Mattie, all made up of glass, brick and stone! So tall they go a hundred feet straight up in the air!"

He pretends he is looking up and up at the imaginary building and playfully leans way back, almost falling over. He snaps up, animated. "Skyscrapers are what my dream angel calls them! So tall, they scrape the sky! Then we drive up to the front door of an elegant restaurant ... to the front door, mind you! The white attendant, all dressed up fancy wearing a top hat walks up and opens the door to our carriage." He mimics the car attendant strutting over to Mattie and opens the imaginary car door with a bow.

Mattie responds in shock. "Glory, glory.... You telling me that a white man opens the door, parks the carriage and brings it to you all when you are ready to leave?"

"Yup, he sure rightly does! Just like the boys that would go fetch the carriages for guests after a fancy white plantation cotillion! The valet opens the door then takes her by the hand and helps her out. He gives us a little bow and a tip of the hat, too!" Jeremiah continues to act out the date for his aunt; pretending to tip the man, Jeremiah struts around, pimp walking to the door as he talks.

Mattie laughs. "My, my, praise the Lord, now ain't that something—a bow and tip of the hat, too?" She imagines with a happy sigh.

"Aunt Mattie, we walk to the door and the doorman opens it for us, too! We step inside the elegant restaurant. White linen tablecloths cover all the tables, decked out with big fancy napkins held by silver rings and real silverware laid out. Beautiful fresh cut flowers are on every table set with the whitest finest gold trim china and crystal glasses. The debonair headwaiter approaches us with one of those big white napkins draped over his left forearm . . . walking like this." Jeremiah grabs a dishtowel and throws it over his arm, mocking the waiter's haughty, uppity approach.

Mattie, caught up in the moment, warns Jeremiah. "Oh, oh, he's coming to tell y'all, 'We don't serve Negros in here who do you think you are sitting down in here!'"

"No, no, Mattie, this is my favorite part of those dreams! This is a different kind of America. They treat us just as free and independent as any white man. Yup, we free to do anything we want in this dream world, Mattie! He places napkins in our laps and hands us menus."

Mattie happily daydreams. "Oh my goodness!"

"We had the most perfect date, ending up riding around in her fancy riding contraption. That's when she taught me how to drive."

Mattie joyfully teases Jeremiah. "Get out! Boy, you and that imagination of yours is something else! My, my you talking about driving one of them fast horseless contraptions. White folks serving black folks.… Now that is what I call a fairy tale if I ever heard one!" Both crack up with laughter, shaking their heads in disbelief at the reality of times he just described ever happening….

The dream made for good entertainment as John and Hope laughed it up hilariously hearing his story. Watching him act out his humorous futuristic fairy tale dream, dumbfounded Angela stood speechless staring at Jeremiah, astonished by the story he had just told. Except for the part about teaching Jeremiah how to drive, he just described her exact dream, the dream of her perfect date with *That Guy* a hundred and a fifty years from now.

With a chuckle, Hope encouraged him. "Jeremiah, with the Emancipation, maybe one day in the distant future the freedom and those dreams will become true!

John jokingly added, displaying a big wide know-it-all smirk on his face, "And who knows, maybe one day this country will even have a black president!"

"Now *that* would truly be a dream come true!" Jeremiah quickly dismissed the fantasy with a chuckle. He turned to Angela.

"Is this just a mere coincidence, us meeting like this, my angel? If so, I am still a lucky man!" His charm caused Angela to blush.

"Why, that's right kindly of you, Jeremiah! What you just shared means a lot to me! Let us call it providence that brings us together!" Her skin flushed with heat. So desperately she wanted to tell him everything of having the same wonderful perfect date and other wonderful dreams of them together! However, she could not. She fought to resist flinging herself right into his big, strong arms with confessions of their paths crossing just like he spoke of. Though it was 1867, Jerimiah Stone was indeed That Guy. The same man of her dreams, whom she falls in love with one hundred and fifty years into the future.

Chapter 8

In Time and On Time

"Aww, come on! For crying out loud! Hope, cowboys, the Civil War, and look what happened to my sword!" He shoved the end of it into Jeremiah's face. "It's time for you all to tell me what's *really* going on around here." John complained loudly. Without saying a word, Hope stepped up and gave Jeremiah a look of apology. She gently took down John's arm.

"Kind sir, could you please excuse us for a moment?"

Pulling John to the side so as not to be overheard, she whispered a shocking revelation.

"He is not Moloch nor be he a vampire!" she snickered. "Everything is all right, John! Yes, you are right about this being Mariah—" She hesitated. "However, we have journeyed to the year 1867."

"Eighteen WHAT? Sixty-seven? Aww naw, naw, Hope. Are you *serious*?"

She pointed out into the fog. "This is all part of our quest. This is where our battle takes place. I already told you that others would join us. Sorry, John, I know it is hard to understand, but you must think twice before you react. This is not in the same Mariah you know."

"You're telling me we have traveled back in time to the year 1867? Oh, my God ... that is almost a hundred and fifty years, Hope! You mean we are back in Mariah right after the Civil War?" John complained belligerently. He was so overwrought his tantrum drew attention from the stranger.

"Shhh ... don't let him hear you!" Hope cautioned, nodding in the stranger's direction.

John looked over at Jeremiah, then back to Hope.

"We will need his help along with the cross here, John, so go over and make friends with him. It will make for more confusion if he knows that we are from the future."

Flustered, he looked at the cross in his hand then over her shoulder to Angela and Jeremiah.

"I hear you!" John replied and headed over to Jeremiah, sulking.

"My name is John, this is Hope, and she is Sherrr . . . er . . . Angela!" He quickly corrected himself. "Are you sure you didn't suffer some kind of head injury during the War, son?" John patronized Jeremiah, regarding his fancy talk of dreams and promises.

"John! Hush!" Angela rolled her eyes in contempt for his disrespectfulness. She turned to Jeremiah. "Praise the Lord and Merry Christmas, my kind sir! Yes, we are visitors to these parts, traveling on an important journey of faith." She took the man's hand and warmly shook it.

"And to each of you a very Merry Christmas, Praise the Lord! So you are missionaries?" Jeremiah humbly replied, admiring her radiant beauty. "Does your quest bring you to Mariah like the Lord has called the rest of us here, my angel?" he asked, squirming and acting foolish, like an infatuated schoolchild. He turned to Hope. He smiled, tipping his hat. "Yeah, one can see very well that you all aren't from around these parts!"

Hope smiled and kindly nodded back at him, acknowledging his compliment. His attention diverted back to Angela's' smiling face.

"Where do you call home, my angel?"

Not allowing Angela to answer, John could not help but rudely interrupt and spoil another moment between the two. "No, no! Look, Afro-man! She is not the angel you recognize her to be. You sure do ask a lot of questions for someone who almost ran down and killed folks minding their own business. Where did you learn to ride that horse, anyway? You need to get a horn or something or at least give a shout out when you ride up on pedestrians like that!" John snapped at the big man. Jerimiah looked puzzled.

"Pedestrians, you say? Is that what you newcomers call yourselves, Pedestrians?" Jeremiah naïvely inquired. "I have heard of Presbyterians and Episcopalians, but I've never heard of any Pedestrians, my good brother. Is this a new type of religion you bring with you to Mariah?"

John condescended, "Pedestrians are *all* people that walk along streets ... I mean roads. So you tell me, my good man, what do you do around here besides galloping through the woods like you just stole something?"

"My name is Jeremiah Stone." Taking John's joking remark seriously and personally, Jeremiah felt as though his manhood was being challenged. Annoyed by his arrogant attitude and being made a mockery of by John, he had had his fill of name-calling and disrespect. He fought the urge to strike him down. He scoffed irritably, openly showing his contempt. "I have already made my apology for what might have been a most tragic accident. I dislike the fact that you attempt to imply that I be a common thief or highway robber of some sort. You should be aware that accusations loosely thrown about such as those you have just made could get a Negro killed around these parts!

"We call this valley God's country and welcome and share hospitality with all emancipated Negros of all religions who find their calling to Mariah. However, mind you, that does not mean we always turn the other cheek to the rude and inconsiderate ones. I ask that from this point on you watch your tongue with me or I will take physical action upon you."

John stepped up to the man towering over him.

"Say what? Was that a threat? So what's up? What you want to do, Negro?" John confronted him, holding the cross in Jeremiah's face again. Jeremiah was about to thrash John when Angela irritably spoke.

"Stop this bickering, you two! Jeremiah, I am so terribly sorry to have to tell you but it is impossible for me to be the same angel! It was wrong for John to imply that you are some kind of a thief. However, I agree with him, you do dress like one! You must admit you do look like some kind of criminal riding around dressed as you are wearing that red scarf over your face! John, stop this behavior and your harsh, childish remarks. Behave yourself." She made her point with pursed lips. "We must be careful of all who may cross our path, for the evil Moloch seek to capture and do us harm. The shadows can deceive to look human. We must protect this precious child from them. Regardless, we all certainly owe you an apology for us assuming that you were of their evil ranks! Please, Jeremiah, understand, John has a tendency to talk too much, ending up with his big feet and ego stuffed in his mouth."

Jeremiah expression changed with her mention of the Moloch clan. He knew well the evil shadows that lurked deep in the mountainous dark woods around Mariah. The whispered ghost stories elder townsfolk told of the missing children, the sacrifice of hearts to the one they praised. They drank their blood and fed on their bodies. The stories were so scary they kept the children out of the woods.

"I know about the evil shadows that wander the woods of Mariah."

Hope pointed to the child and asked Jeremiah, "Please, we must find sanctuary where the child can be safe and protected!"

He looked at Angela and Hope standing with their golden swords strapped to their sides. He wanted to believe in his heart and soul that Angela was the same angel that saved his life that day on the battlefield and in his dreams. He had his doubts about John, however. He looked at the baby Easter, then to Angela, and hoped for the right answer to the question he was about to ask her. Angela anticipated what he was about to say.

"No, she is not my child. Her protection is my charge."

He looked over to John and smiled knowingly.

"Don't look at me, man," John said defensively.

"John is also the child's protector. That is the only relationship he and I have." Jeremiah covered his face with his hat in a boyish manner in order to hide his giant teddy bear smile of glee.

"Yes! Thank you, Jesus!" he spoke into his hat. Looking down shyly, surprise replaces his elated smile. His eyes widen, noticing the tops of John's fancy white shoes, which stuck out from beneath his black friar's frock.

"OH ... Jesus ... excuse me, can I have a look at them?" He pointed down to the amazing shoes. "Where in God's name did you get shoes like that, my good fellow?" He could not take his eyes off the outlandish pair.

John smiled and lifted up his robe to show them off.

"Bet you never laid eyes on a pair of these! You like them, don't you!" John boasted, flaunting his high top basketball shoes, posing in athletic stances.

"May I touch them?" Jeremiah asked, feeling the shoe. "It is like leather. But it is white."

Doing the man thing admiring the shoes helped to change the tense atmosphere.

Hope frowned at John and shoved a sharp elbow into his side. John, realizing his mistake, quickly covered his shoes and avoided the question.

"Listen, let's just forget about my shoes, Jeremiah. I already told you that we are not from around here. You know, shoes are different where we Pedestrians come from!"

Angela joins the conversation. "Jeremiah, the shoes are of no concern right now. What is more important is whether you can join us and help find us sanctuary. Getting the child out of these woods to somewhere that is safe is our immediate need. Please, we can use your help."

"Folks are just plain and simple round here, and they kind of like sticking to themselves. I got to tell you, folks are going to get real antsy with you bringing up talk about the Moloch!" He inspected them all. "You all sure likely to get a lot of people riled up just by the way you all look! Soon as they see the three of you they going to know you all aren't from around here, I can guarantee you that! You being new to these parts will be enough for them to know for now. Come, I will take you over to our church for safety. Reverend Bishop will know what to do."

"Reverend James Bishop?" John said, referring to his own pastor in future Mariah.

"Do you mean Reverend Joshua Bishop? You know or have heard of our good Reverend?" Jeremiah asked.

"No, no! My bad! Uhhhh, I mean, mistake," John replied, cautiously looking at Hope.

"We would like very much to meet him, Jeremiah," Angela said

Confused, John blurted out, "I can't even imagine what's coming up next, Hope!"

"Reverend Bishop?" Hope answered.

The time travelers follow Jeremiah through the woods. Hope walked up beside Jeremiah to speak with him.

"Jeremiah, I've been thinking about what you said back there and I agree with you. For now, we are just people traveling in peace seeking temporary sanctuary for the child and ourselves. All will be revealed today—who we are, along with the truth of what is about to occur, when the time is right."

Jeremiah amicably agreed, not really understanding her true meaning. "Like my Auntie Mattie would say, "The best kept secret is one never spoken. She also likes to say that anything is possible if you have enough hope and faith." He smiled optimistically at Angela.

Listening in on their conversation, Angela silently agreed with his aunt's wisdom, having secrets of her own pertaining to That Guy Jeremiah.

They stopped at the edge of the foggy woods. The three stared in awe at the black folks of generations past gathered in the clearing. They observed the people working vigorously at completing the construction of the large church. They attended this same church in the future Mariah.

Strangely, only a blanket of fog covered the ground. John figured well over a hundred people filled the area. Men working up in the steeple tower prepared to hoist the church bell into it. The women were preparing for the celebration, cooking or minding the children; inside the church they were setting places at the tables.

"Most of the townspeople are here helping with the completion of the church for the christening and dedication celebration tonight. It might be best to put away your weapons and the cross. We can wrap them in this blanket and hide them on Maribel so as not to alarm anyone." Jeremiah wisely suggested.

John, Hope and Angela looked at each other and reluctantly agreed.

"You mentioned the minister's name is Reverend Joshua Bishop?" Hope asked as he secured the covered weapons and cross on the side of his horse.

"Yes, Reverend Joshua Bishop was called upon by the Lord to come here to Mariah six months ago. He brought with him a large group of orphaned children displaced by the ravages of the Civil War. He told us that this church would be a sanctified sanctuary, a place blessed by the Lord. He anointed this whole valley 'God's Country.'"

"Amen to that!" Hope replied.

"Let's go and meet the good preacher." Jeremiah pointed out the robed man standing in the back of a wagon near the front of the church. The group emerged from the foggy woods. As they stepped into the clearing, a cold brisk wind swept away the mist covering the ground, exposing a large field containing a cemetery filled with unmarked white crosses.

"Newcomers!" An armed man walking guard near the edge of the woods shouted to the other townsfolk.

CHAPTER 9

The Honorable Reverend Joshua Bishop

The townsfolk stop working, delighted by the arrival of 'newcomers.' They waved excitedly to the strangers, shouting out friendly welcomes and holiday greetings as they approached. The sight of the church standing majestically in the middle of the clearing and the dress of the townspeople really hit home for the three strangers. They actually *had* traveled back in time to Mariah nearly a century and a half to the same church they would attend in modern day Mariah! The almost completed church gave them a reverent feeling of a sanctified haven.

"Good morning and Merry Christmas to you, Jeremiah. I see you have brought newcomers to our valley. God bless you all and welcome to Mariah, God's country." The Reverend greeted them, smiling with glee from atop the wagon.

"Good morning and a very Merry Christmas to you, Reverend Bishop," Jeremiah joyously replied. Hope, Angela and John return the good reverend's greeting while they marvel at just how much his future great, great grandson James will resemble the man.

"Have you been staying out of trouble, son?" the Reverend asked as he stepped down from the wagon, looking at the women with Jeremiah.

"As much as a poor freedman can these days of Reconstruction, Reverend!" His remark released some "amens'" and chuckles from the curious crowd of onlookers. The visitors, being the focus of everyone's attention, stood uncomfortably, their hooded robes covering their heads. The locals start to fret, mumbling whispers of witchery, something Jeramiah had not predicted.

The Reverend frowned sternly as the rumbling crowd began to get loud and unruly. He placed a friendly arm around Jeremiah. Acknowledging the three visitors, he asked, "So who have you here, Jeremiah?"

"Well, Rev—" The reverend's brow furrowed, upset by Jeremiah's nickname for him.

"They are missionaries and newfound friends I just met. Well, to be honest, I almost ran them down on the road as they walked in the thick fog on the trail back a ways. They came to visit us from the west, seeking refuge and sanctuary for the night!" Adding missionaries to their profile, he presented the trio proudly to the gathered town folk.

"Wonderful! They're just in time for our christening celebration tonight!" The reverend opened his arms wide.

"They call themselves pedestrians, Reverend Bishop." John shot Jeremiah an angry frown. His scowling brought more unwanted attention from those watching closely.

Jeremiah, taking the hint from John, tried to clear things up.

"I mean, they are called pedestrians when they travel on their missions of mercy!"

"What's a pedestrian?" a woman asked.

A feeble, half-blind old man with gray cataracts stepped out of the crowd.

"In all my born days I can't recollect hearing of such a religion!" Old Leotis Scott was his name. "Let me get a good look at them," he demanded, squinting. His eyes opened wide with fear seeing the three dressed in black monk robes. He drew back.

Feeling the crowd's uneasiness growing, Hope stepped up to allow the old man to scrutinize her as much as he felt necessary. The Reverend intervened and quickly stepped between Hope and the old man.

"Welcome to Mariah, friends. I am Reverend Joshua Bishop. I have also journeyed such as you. Mine led me here to Mariah, and it was here I found my calling."

"Thank you for your warm welcome, Reverend. I am Hope Matthews. It is with much pleasure that we meet you. However, I must correct Jeremiah. Our religion is not pedestrian, as he has mistakenly stated. Pedestrian is a term we use where we come from for people that walk alongside the streets and roads."

The wind rose, blowing Hope's hair over her face as she reached out and firmly shook the reverend's rough hands.

"I am familiar with the term and well aware of Jeremiah's misinterpretation of you."

Relieved, Hope continued with the conversation, speaking loud enough for the crowd.

"We are seeking temporary sanctuary and shelter as we make our way. Jeremiah has been so kind as to suggest you may be able to help us."

Many folks nodded in acceptance while others still whispered suspicious judgments. John stepped forward to address the reverend but before he could speak, Angela took command of the situation. In her booming, authoritative police-officer tone, she spoke from her mount.

"My name is Angela Solomon. As Hope stated, we ask only for temporary shelter and sanctuary. There is nothing to fear from us. We offer our services and our help in any way that we can provide! We travel in peace. We do not pass judgment on others without reason! We do unto others as we would want upon ourselves!"

The crowd was stunned, intimidated by her strong, in-charge tone. At hearing her name, Reverend Bishop looked admirably at her.

"Angela Solomon, you say? What a strong, spiritual name you've been given, my child."

"Why, thank you, Reverend." Nodding and bowing respectfully, her odd, colorful braids fell out from underneath her hood. Loud gasps came from the crowd as she quickly pushed them back underneath.

"She's a witch!" a female voice frightfully called out.

"There will not be any more of that!" the Reverend responded, frowning at the outburst. He turned to Angela and smiled.

"Well, now, let's see that hair of yours, girl, you don't have to hide anything around here. We are all Gods' children and, as you so eloquently put it, we have nothing to fear from you all. So let me take a look at that beautiful hair of yours."

Angela pushed back her hood, flinging her head proudly in order for everyone to see her two big, beautiful red and blue braids. Some people were frightened and leery of Angela's bold display. Nevertheless, most of them became excited, wanting to learn more about the strange newcomers. The Reverend quelled the crowd.

"Your braids are beautiful, my dear lady. As with all newcomers, we welcome you all to Mariah. We came to this place for a purpose not yet known other than that we are here by the Lord's will. This may very well be your case. However, I don't recall anyone that's here with the special purpose to pass judgment on welcomed visitors!" He gave the chattering crowd a concerned look. Then, noticing John's strange shoes, he could not hold back his question, "May I take a look at your boots, son?"

John reluctantly raised his robe so the reverend could better examine the modern high top Nikes. Gasps mixed with oohs and ahhs, sprung again from those gathered around.

"By the way, son, I have to ask, where in God's name did you purchase the magnificent white boots on your feet there? Was this the cobbler's name, 'Nickees' and his artisan mark here on the side? Is this white leather?"

Everyone waited with much anticipation for John's answer. The three visitors looked at each other. A loud cracking sound interrupted from above. Everyone looked up to see the main rigging snap from the weight of the bell hoisted up halfway to the steeple. The heavy iron bell slammed to the ground with a muffled bong. The snapped rigging rocketed dangerously toward a woman standing directly in its path. She screamed as the T-beam miraculously changed direction and impaled itself into the ground, landing a few feet in front of her. The rigging looked like a slanted, upside down crucifix.

All attention shifted from the strangers to the woman. Reverend Bishop ran over to her.

"Thank you, Lord! She is unharmed! It is a miracle. It was truly the hand of God that saved you!" Making sure she was all right, he turned to the bell on the ground.

"Please, Lord, show us more of Your mercy. Please let it not be damaged!"

During the confusion, Jeremiah whispered to the visitors.

"Maybe it is best we all leave now. Come on, we have got to go, you all are starting too much commotion around here! " As the troupe slipped away back into the foggy woods, Jeremiah stopped.

"My uncle and aunt are owners of the general store in town. We can get you all some clothes to replace your robes so as not to draw as much attention."

He turned to John, pointing at his shoes.

"Brother, you might want to think about giving up those shoes. They draw too much attention."

Angela was quick to respond. "You're right, Jeremiah."

Hope also acknowledged, nodding approvingly.

They all wait for John's response; however, he was not as anxious to give up his new Air Jordans as suggested.

"I'll have to think about that one ... maybe when I see some proper replacements, Jeremiah! Let's go see what your uncle and aunt have to offer. Hopefully they will be able to hook us up proper, my brother!"

Jeremiah laughed aloud as John's slang soaked in. "'Hook us up'! That is another new one on me. Ha! The boy's use of English words gives me good humor when he is not disrespectful. These newcomers are all quite different."

The crowd buzzed from the arrival and sudden disappearance of Jeremiah and the newcomers. Everyone had something to say about the three strangers and all that had happened once they appeared out of the woods. The main topic most talked about was the miracle of the woman saved from sure death.

Reverend Bishop returned inside the church, climbing up into the steeple to assess the damage. Meanwhile, for everyone standing around, the newcomers seemed just too damn different. They acted too independent, more entitled and more uppity than *"house Negros."* They seemed to come from a world apart.

"Strange that they would sneak off and leave like that," a woman standing nearby named Kimberly Ann said. "Did you notice how she tried to hide her strange-colored hair at first? I looked into her eyes and she possessed a very high and mighty attitude. You could tell they weren't from anywhere around these parts."

A bitter, much older very dark-hued woman named Mae Mayfield added fuel to the fire. She directed her angry voice to the crowd.

"They never did say exactly where they were from. Have you ever seen anybody wearing red and blue braids or shoes like that?" She continued her rant against the newcomers. "Funny, too, did you notice that just when the good reverend began asking questions about that boy's strange shoes, the steeple bell fell so they could sneak back into the woods with Jeremiah?"

The crowd grew silent. Leery and suspicious of the newcomers from the get go, Old man Leotis spoke out boldly against the strangers, "And what about those strange white shoes the quiet young man had on? He did not speak a single word the whole time. Who here has ever seen some white shoes like that? Humph! Why do they dress the way they do? Did you all notice that woman on the horse was carrying something wrapped up in that bundled up blanket she held in her lap? I gets a funny feeling they were either hiding or running from something! They are the strangest bunch of missionary people that I've ever come across!" Leotis fueled the growing bonfire of suspicion even more. "The bible tells us to beware of false prophets! Why did they sneak off like that? Did you see how nervous the boy got when the reverend asked about where those shoes came from? I just do not like or trust these newcomers; there's something very strange about them! Mark my words!"

"Oh, shut up, you old fool!" An angry Gail Finney stepped up in defense of the absent strangers. She was one of the younger, newly appointed church matrons. "I did not see anything wrong with the newcomers! In fact, I felt reverence in their company! Now, what you got to say about that, Mister Leotis?" She challenged the crowd.

Lottie joined the ranks. "Just 'cause we look a little different or talk a little different don't make us no different, we all the same. I am going to pray for you, Leotis! I do not like your accusations you make against the newcomers. I feel no threats or fear of them."

Taking offense, Leotis rebutted, "There you young people go again! What do you young people know anyhow? What you both need to do is listen and respect your elders and as an elder, I can say or give my opinion of whatever I feel because we free now. I have seen a lot in my day and they something all right, but they are not plain ordinary Negroes. I get a bad feeling about them pesdestrians!"

"Oh, Leotis, you needs to shut up!" Lottie Roberts stepped up again in defense of the strangers. "What kind of people would you say they were then, Leotis?"

Unbeknownst to everyone, just as Leotis stated, they were all soon to see that the newcomers were very far from ordinary.

CHAPTER 10

The Matthews

I n current-day Mariah, the winter wind howled outside in the morning darkness. A frantic knock banged against the kitchen back door at the home of Faith and Rosemary Matthews. It was early Christmas Eve morning. Anticipating that it was her beloved fiancé, John, Faith Matthews, already wide-awake with worry, jumped up out of bed and ran downstairs to the back of the house.

She turned on the kitchen lights and anxiously looked out the back door curtained window. Two female figures stepped into the light.

"Hurry up and open this door, child, it's your aunts, Ruth and Esther. It is cold out here!" Both unveiled their shawls to show their faces.

"Hurry up and open this door baby girl!" Faith recognized her sweet Aunt Ruth. Standing next to her sister, Esther complained loudly, crinkling her nose and sniffing the air.

"Child, come on and open this door.... I can smell evil out here in the air!" She nervously checked behind her. Faith hurriedly unlocked the door and greeted them with huge hugs. Both were bundled up, quivering, more out of fear than from the early morning frost.

"Merry Christmas, Aunt Ruth, Aunt Esther! This is sure going to be quite a Christmas surprise for Momma!"

"Praise the Lord we made it. Quick, child, lock that door." Shuddering, they rushed into the house.

Standing at the top of the staircase, awakened by the noise from downstairs, Rosemary hollered down to Faith. "Who is that down there making all that commotion this early in the morning, Faith? And it better not be John coming over here with none of his foolishness at this hour!"

"MA, IT'S AUNTIES!" Faith shouted. Rosemary, hearing that the unexpected visitors were her adorable older holy-rolling sisters, Esther and Ruth McGinnis, she was instantly overjoyed. It was the fraternal twin's first visit back home to Mariah in twelve long years.

Rosemary then became worried and alarmed. "Oh, my God, what are they doing here?"

The sisters put their overnight bags down, immediately bowing their heads. Esther gave thanks.

"Thank you, Lord, and thank you, Jesus, for bringing us home safely!" both prayed aloud.

"A*MEN* to that!" Rosemary hollered, rushing into the kitchen to greet them.

"Oh, my Lord ... Ruth and Esther here in Mariah? Well I'll be, thank you, Jesus!" Rosemary declared with tears of joy in her eyes.

"Sit down rest yourselves! I'll put some hot tea on." It had been too long since she last enjoyed the company of her older twin sisters in her home. The sisters unbundled themselves and tried to get comfortable.

"Merry Christmas!" both blandly respond in unison.

"Why didn't you call and let us know you were coming? You two know better than to be traveling around these parts alone, especially at night! What are you two doing back here in Mariah, anyway?" Her furrowed brow and frown turned into a blissful welcoming smile.

No longer able to hold back the joy of having them back, Rosemary grabbed them both together and bear hugged then tightly in her big arms. "Come here, Merry Christmas, you two!"

The sisters were not in a very celebrating mood. Tipped off by their solemn silence, Rosemary immediately knew it could only mean trouble was brewing on the horizon.

"We have been called back and it doesn't have anything to do with no celebrating!" The twins responded, very unenthusiastically, again in unison. Ruth got right to the point.

"We received the calling that it was time to return to Mariah. The evil growing here is like never before. You are going to need our help to deal with this one and we got no intentions of staying around once we are done with our business."

"Not a minute longer, Lord!" Esther confirmed.

The day passed slowly as the women tried to occupy themselves with chatter. That night, Ruth and Esther could barely sleep. Cold, howling winds swirled around the house, rattling doors and beating against their windows. They prayed and cowered under bedcovers, shaking in their beds and praying as strange sounds in the night thumped and bumped inside the walls and underneath the floor.

"Ezekiel Joppa himself has arrived!" Aunt Ruth whispered, terrified.

"I know! I can feel his evil presence, too! As soon as we are done with this, we're outta here!" Esther whispered back.

* * *

The Matthews family gathered on Christmas morning, edgy and weary from the rough night. Ruth led them in prayer.

"Thank you, Lord, for providing protection over us through the night."

"And for protecting us from everything that hides within it!" Faith added.

"Amen to that!" The aunts responded in unison.

"We brought something special for you, Faith," the aunts said together, excitedly. "We've decided while we are here to make your wedding gown!"

Ruth pulled out the sewing pattern from the oversized pockets of her thick, terry cloth robe. She carefully unfolded it, showing Faith the beautiful picture of the elegant silk satin wedding gown. Faith's eyes lit up, dancing with joy and delight. She kissed them on the cheek and squealed with joy, hugging them both.

"Oh, Aunties, you both are the best! It' so beautiful!!" .

The attempt to bring some Christmas cheer into the home lasted only a short while. The moment was spoiled when Faith turned on the television, which was broadcasting emergency disaster weather reports of the strange storms plaguing the northeastern coastline.

They continued to watch in silence. Getting no sleep after her sisters' arrival, Rosemary was tired and weary from praying all night. She fell fast asleep on the couch.

Esther, having had her fill of what she was watching, said, "Turn it off, I've seen enough of it! We already know what is happening! And it ain't got nothing to do with the weather!"

"Esther's right, that's enough watching that mess. Come on baby, I am so happy we brought this dress. It is going to take our minds right off of all this evil stuff going on! Come on—while we got the time, let's start the fitting!"

Loud snores erupted from the couch, interrupting the joy-filled moment.

"Ha-ha! You know your momma's been snoring like that since she was twelve!" Ruth lovingly complained.

"She still isn't as loud as you!" Esther quipped.

"Well look at the pot calling the skillet black! You snore louder than the both of us!" Ruth retaliated.

They all laughed as Faith shook her head, amused by her aunts' bickering. It brought to mind memories of her own exchanges of sibling rivalry with Hope. Noticing a sudden chill fill the room, Faith retrieved a warm quilt and covered Rosemary with it. She kissed her lovingly on the forehead. Retreating upstairs to begin the fitting, Faith took a doting look back at her sleeping mother. Listening to her boisterous snorting and wheezing, she could not imagine anyone snoring as loud as her Momma!

The three proceeded upstairs to Faith's bedroom and stood in front of the large beautiful three-paneled full-length mirror. The family heirloom stood six-and-a-half feet tall and six-feet wide. Inlaid with jade, the black, high-gloss walnut wood frame and back panels were hand designed with odd oriental markings carved into the wood. The sight of it instantly brought smiles to Ruth and Esther, reminiscing on all the good times they spent as children playing dress up for hours in front of the mirror in their parent's bedroom.

"Something bothers me. I should be able to sense your fiancé's spirit like a beacon in the dark, my dear! So how is it I feel only our four spirits in Mariah?" Ruth bluntly questioned her niece.

Faith understood the reason for the question, feeling the same absence of her lover's spirit. Intimidated by her aunt's remarks, Faith defiantly defended her absent fiancé.

"Oh, don't worry about my man, he will be here today and once you meet him, you will see how righteous my fiancé is!"

Esther snapped at Faith's pretentious remarks. "Did you hear the tone she just used with us, Ruth?"

"You need to climb down off that high horse you're riding on right now, young lady! Show your aunties some respect!" Ruth scolded, backing her sister.

"And, for your information, I can question anything I want of you, young lady—we're family like that and I'm your elder, thank you very much!"

"All Esther asked was where was he? Your fiancé one should have been part of the calling here meeting with us right now this with all that is about to start! To be truthful with you, honey, I cannot feel his presence around here, either! Sister is right. If he is here in Mariah, we all should be able to feel his spirit. Now, do not get us wrong, we are concerned about his absence because he should be here with us!"

"You right about that!" Esther confirmed. The two sisters nodded knowingly to each other and returned to fitting the wedding dress in silence. Faith's anxiety grew.

Lord, John, where are you? I need you here!

Outdoors, a thick fog consumed the house. Faith's body began to tremble as the scent of sulfur filled the room. Ruth, kneeling on the floor in front of her, felt evils approach. She looked fearfully over to her sister. Their attention was drawn toward the mirror as it began to glow. They stared as the glass on the other side billowed with black clouds. The straight pins in Ruth's open mouth dropped to the floor as she found it impossible to let out a scream.

Ezekiel Joppa emerged from the darkness, black wings wrapped around his body. Faith, upon seeing the image, began to shake and sweat profusely. The wings slowly opened, revealing two lifeless babies cradled in his arms. The babies' eyes suddenly opened, revealing angry, grey cat-like eyes.

Recognizing Ruth and Esther, he screamed like a banshee. "How dare you return here!" Turning, he yelled to someone they could not see. "Go tell Father the banished ones have returned here! The sisters have returned to Mariah."

The mirror overflowed as more lost souls flew out of the mist behind them to get a look at the women, terrified, on the other side of the mirror.

"Capture them all! The witch's death is the price they pay for their return here!" Heavy thuds crashed against the thick-mirrored glass as larger demons tried to break through to get at the women. It took all of Faith's might and will to cry out.

"MOMMA!"

She fainted, dropping to the floor like a stone, falling right on top of Ruth in front of the mirror.

Esther stood by the dresser, petrified. She was holding on tightly to the bible in her hands.

"God is in the midst of me and I shall not be moved!"

Struggling, she finally was able to grab hold of the vial of holy water on the dresser. Repeating the prayer, she poured a few drops into her hands, allowing her to move freely. She rushed to her sister's side, splashing a few drops on her forehead, releasing her from evil's grip.

"Get up; they are coming to kill us, Esther!"

Before she could get to Faith, one of the babies' arms passed through the now-glowing glass. Licking its lips, it grabbed hold of Faith's foot, pulling her body toward the mirror. The other evil little twin helped, quickly taking hold of her legs.

"They are trying to take her!" Esther screamed. They grabbed hold of Faith's arms. "Her body must not pass through the mirror or the portal will open and they will take us all to hell! Hold on!" Ruth yelled.

Ruth released Faith's arm and ran up to the front of the mirror. She began to stomp on the little arms, causing the babies to release their grip on Faith's feet. They screamed, letting go and rearing back in pain. The other creatures went berserk at this effrontery. They charged to the front and pounded heavily against the mirror in anger.

Ruth turned her back to the mirror and pulled Faith's legs out. In doing so, one of the babies reached through and swiped its sharp talons across her buttocks.

"Ahhhhgggh!" Screaming in pain, Ruth grabbed hold of her butt, falling unconscious next to Faith.

Esther stepped in between them and the mirror. She stomped down hard, crushing the deformed baby hands with her foot. Screeching in pain, the babies quickly flew back into the winged arms of Ezekiel.

"You dare harm my babies? I will kill you myself!" he hollered, flying toward the mirror.

Esther ran over to the dresser, grabbing a crucifix and shouting to the images in front of her, "In the name of God Almighty, I rebuke you and all your evilness. We returned to Mariah in defiance of you. The battle begins!" She hurled the crucifix, destroying the mirror.

Looking at the large shards of broken glass, they watched as the gathered hordes of vile demons ran back into the fading black clouds and the reflective glass became clear once more.

Downstairs, Rosemary slowly awakened from her own nightmare. Her body was soaking wet from sweat. She heard the loud crashing of glass coming from upstairs. She grabbed her chest and looked around the empty living room.

"FAITH! RUTH? ESTHER!" Getting no answer, she got up from the couch, moving as fast as she could down the hallway to the stairs.

She felt her heart pounding against her chest at a dangerously demanding pace. Sweat dripped off her face as she struggled to climb up the staircase leading to her daughter's bedroom.

"Oh, my God ... no!" Her heart was about to explode.

"Not now, Lord, please don't take me, not now." she prayed softly. She leaned against the wall as she walked down the hallway to keep from falling. Her left arm went numb. Rosemary, entering into her daughter's room, held back her scream seeing everyone laid out on the floor and broken pieces of glass everywhere. She covered her mouth and nose from the stench of sulfur that filled the air.

"Oh, Lord! My baby!" she screamed and leaned against the dresser to get a second wind. Esther sat up on the floor next to Faith, exhausted. Ruth lay on her stomach, wounded, moaning.

"We been attacked, Rosemary! Faith is all right! They came to open the gate and take us all to hell … it was Ezekiel." She pointed to the broken mirror.

Esther finished. "They came after us to face the witch's death for coming back to Mariah! But we showed them! Baby sister? Rosemary, are you all right?"

"Yes, I'm fine, sister, thanks to Jesus!"

Getting a second wind, Rosemary picked up Faith, who was still unconscious. She held her child in her arms.

"Can you walk on your own, Ruth? Let's leave out of here, this room stinks of sulfur and evil."

* * *

All were having a hard time fully recovering from the attack by the powerful evil paranormal forces they confronted upstairs in Faith's bedroom. Rosemary sat on the couch staring at her unconscious daughter cradled in her arms. Esther has tended to Ruth's injury. They sat in sullen silence watching the local news report on the recent weather disasters, knowing it marked Ezekiel's return to Mariah.

"I wonder why John is not here with us." Rosemary voiced her concern.

"Now do you understand the reason why we have returned to Mariah?" Ruth exclaimed, stressed.

"He is more powerful than before!" Esther added, fanning with a newspaper.

Faith's eyes suddenly opened, filled with terror. She screamed hysterically in her mothers' face, struggling to get up. Rosemary held on tightly and tried to calm her.

"It's okay, baby ... Momma's here ... it's okay."

"I saw her, Momma! I had visions of the dead church burner Edward Troy's wife Helen returning leading the Moloch clan in battle against us! An evil revenging ... female in a chariot of fire ... will join forces with them and they are coming, coming here to kill me! I saw my own death, Momma!" It was the same dream Rosemary was having downstairs while sleeping on the couch.

Hearing this, Ruth moaned and squinted in pain as she moved to change her sitting position.

"Owww! You ain't the only one they're after child, and a big battle is coming, you better believe that!" She quipped, gently rubbing her buttocks.

They sat again in uncomfortable silence as the adults waited for Faith to step up. Faith did not respond. Her aunties were disappointed. Esther, unsettled by Faith's hesitation and behavior, whispered to Ruth.

"Look at her big grown butt sitting over there whimpering in her mother's safe arms like a little ol' baby! Lucky for her I'm a child of the Lord ... Oooh, I could just snatch her!" she scathed.

"Whew, I'm thirsty! Esther, can you please hand me a glass that of that holy water?" Rosemary asked. Esther complied.

She drank, then asked for another.

"Here, baby, take a drink of this."

"I—I'm not thirsty, Momma." Faith reacted and tries to pull away from her strong mother's grip.

"Come on, honey. Here, just take a little sip for Momma!"

Rosemary took a strong hold of Faith, forcing the cup to her lips and pouring the water in her mouth. She then threw the rest of the glass of water into her face.

Faith screamed in agony, struggling desperately to break free from her mother's strong grasp.

"With the blood of Jesus I command you to show your evil wickedness that possesses my daughter. Leave her spirit and body now ... I expel you in the name of the Lord!"

Rosemary hugged Faith tightly as violent seizures twisted and turned her daughter's body. Ruth and Esther began to pray.

Faith let out an excruciating scream and slumped into her mother's hugging arms, knocked out cold.

A hissing shadow of a dark spirit rises above them out from the girl's body. With a distorted male voice, the ghastly face of Ezekiel Joppa appeared and threatened them.

"Get ready to meet your death, you bunch of old fools!" The image disappeared.

Rosemary laid Faith on the couch. She soaked cotton swabs in holy water, cleaning the scratches on Faith's legs and feet.

"When you told me she was touched by the evil children I knew they placed the darkness inside of her. His deceptions are more diabolical than ever...."

Rosemary then suddenly blurted out, "Oh my Lord, where is my mind? I need to call Reverend Bishop about all this!"

As Rosemary reached to use the phone, it rang.

"Hello?" she answered.

"Hello, Rosemary? It's Reverend James Bishop calling. It is important that I get in touch with John Davidson. Have you seen him?"

"Reverend, we were wondering about the boy, too. No one has seen or heard from him. We need both of you here. I was just about to call y—" the Reverend interrupted.

"I envisioned it happening again. It has begun, Rosemary, and we must prepare. I need the altar cross John keeps in his possession to help us defend against the evil that is here!"

"Reverend, listen. We've already been attacked over here inside my house by no other than Ezekiel Joppa! He has returned! As I was saying, I was just about to call you. We need your guidance and prayers and if possible for you to come over here right now! We need to keep trying to get in touch with John," she urgently requests, her voice a mixture of anxiety and worry.

"You know why he has returned to Mariah, don't you, Rosemary? Our end nears." His voice sounded distant and bleak. His drunken undertone raised goose bumps on her arms. Hesitantly, she whispered in anguish back into the phone.

"Oh, my God, Reverend, Faith and I just had the same visions of the end of everything! She had—" Reverend Bishop rudely interrupted her again.

"Don't you see, the Moloch have returned to Mariah to kill us all Rosemary! It was never over . . . never! We might have won the last battle, but they come to seek personal vengeance upon us now!" Static interrupted the phone conversation.

"Rosemary?"

"Hello? Reverend Bishop? Hello? Speak up! I can't hear you!"

The sound of a million angry bees fills the earpieces of both phones, terrifying Rosemary and the Reverend. She threw the receiver down, covering her bleeding ear in pain, pointing frantically at the phone lying on the floor. She screamed to her sister in terror.

"Esther, hang up that phone. Hurry up! Hang it up before the demons get out!"

PART TWO

STANDING AT THE CROSSROADS

CHAPTER 11

Let's Hook 'em Up!

While the Matthews faced incredible challenges of their own in the future, the trio in the past stood inside Mariah's General Store with Jeremiah. He was busy explaining to his aunt and uncle about the newcomers' arrival.

"You should have seen all the excitement stirred up at the church by those shoes!"

Mattie and Seth looked the strangers over. Turning back to their nephew, they both raised their eyebrows in the same way—they do say married folks start looking alike after being together for a long time.

"They do look pretty out of place to me! Just look at that one's hair, and those black robes, Seth!" Mattie observed.

"Just who are they supposed to be again?" the Uncle whispered.

"Well, the strangers are traveling on a special personal quest. They call themselves pedestrians."

"Quest?… Pedestrians, you say? I ain't ever heard of any religion called that before!" Seth remarked.

"That's what I said, Unk, when I first heard it. They all are kind of different!"

"A pedestrian is what they call people who walk along a street or road, not a religion. I used to hear the word spoken all the time in New York City."

"Auntie, there's one more thing I got to tell you! The woman over there holding the child … I know her."

"What? Boy, I hope you not saying what I think you saying?" Seth grimaced.

"My oh my, Jeremiah!" Mattie groaned loudly. "Don't tell me that you done went and had a baby without telling nobody!"

"No, no, aww, come now, you two, I didn't mean I know her like that! My angel I always talk to you about, Mattie! The angel in my dreams—she looks exactly like the angel that came and saved my life that blessed day."

"Oh, my, my … really?" Mattie was excited, caught up in the moment. *Such beautiful dreams! I hope he hasn't already scared the wits out of the poor girl with his … imaginations!*

"Mattie!" Seth snapped, bringing her out of her daydreaming state of mind. He threw Jeremiah a questionable look and sniffed his face.

"Have you been drinking, son? You know we tolerate no drinking around here!"

"I ain't had no spirits, Unk!" Jeremiah defended himself.

Mattie's excitement quickly faded to disappointment. As much as she wanted to believe he had found his angel, she now feared that maybe he had totally lost his ever-loving mind! Mattie nervously wrung her hands. Looking over at Seth doubtfully, she said, "Are you sure she is the woman you always talking about?"

"Yeah, I'm sure it's her!"

"That sure is a lot to chew on, Jeremiah, telling us all this at once like this. Making such claims about them, makes me want to think more on it and get to know them better. Not that they may not be telling the truth, mind you." She pushed her glasses up on her nose, carefully studying the women.

"They sure are beautiful gals, even though they do seem a bit, I guess, the words 'out of place' would be the best way to describe it. There's something different about them. They seems to be sweet and proper young women, though, no?"

Seth suggested, "I think it would make it more comfortable for everyone if they rid themselves of those black robes, don't you think? And excuse me for saying, Mattie, but like you said, they sure are pretty!" Mattie's shot him a stern look. Seth changed his admiring expression, duly chastened.

"Yeah, they are special, Unk! And like you said, they need to rid themselves of the robes! Come and take a look at the child, she is very special, too!"

"I don't know about this." Grabbing tight hold of her husband's arm, Mattie hesitated. Jeremiah took them up to the front of the store toward Angela and the child.

"The boy claims the child you hold is special. May we take a look at her, young miss?" Seth asked Angela.

"Of course you may!" Smiling, she welcomed the request and unwrapped the robe for them to see. They looked upon the sleeping child, taking witness to her reverence. The child smiled and giggled in her sleep. Seth was the first to speak.

"My Lord, she is indeed a precious child." He uttered the words in almost a whisper.

"The child is blessed.... Praise the Lord." Mattie agreed. Hands cupped over her face, she smiled as tears of joy filled her eyes.

"You all make yourselves right at home. Whatever you need, just ask," Seth offered.

Mattie took charge.

"Ladies, come over here with me. I just got some new dresses in from New York I want you to see. I know since the war, dresses are a luxury. I haven't been able to sell one in months. It is hard times everywhere, especially when it comes to us colored folks, but decent women should not be out wearing men's pants and shirts. That is, unless they got more man than woman in them," Mattie commented, admiring the vibrant colors and feeling the fine, modern clothing. "But, now, I do like these flannel shirts you gals are wearing.

The child awoke, hungry.

"The baby could use some milk, if you have it," Angela asked.

"I got a goat out back in the shed, if that's all right?"

"That'll do fine," Angela said.

Mattie grabbed a large tin cup and stepped out the back door for a few minutes, returning with the cup full of milk for the child. As Angela feds the baby, Mattie stared, admiring the two fancy braids she wore.

"You all sure are some pretty gals. You'd best be careful traveling around these parts." Mattie turned to Hope and asked, "Where do you all come from and where does your quest take you?"

"It's a small town a lot like this one, ma'am," Hope cautiously told her.

"Please, call me Mattie. What did you say the name of your town was?" Mattie pressed further. Hope and Angela, caught off guard by this question, looked awkwardly at each other.

"Please don't take it personally, but for the protection of the child, where we come from and where we travel must be kept secret. The child is in great danger!"

Finally, breaking the uncomfortable moments of silence, Mattie smiled.

"Well, that's good enough for me, child. Do not mind me; I can be a nosy old woman when I want to. I didn't mean to pry! Tell me no more. My momma always told me the best-kept secret is one never spoken. No one with thoughts of harming that child will be welcome here. Are you sure you are not hungry? Looks as if you can use a little meat on them bones.

Big Jeremiah and John, hearing Mattie's offer to feed the women, responded, "I AM!"

"When aren't you hungry, Jeremiah?" Mattie's joke made everyone laugh. Hope said, "No, thank you, Mattie, but it looks like you have enough on your hands feeding him!"

"Seth, fetch them boys some jerky. We should get you all back over to the church celebration. They will have plenty of food to eat there and we need to talk to the reverend!"

Mattie turned back to the young women.

"Well now, how about I get you something different to put on."

Hope apologized, "No disrespect, ma'am, but we would rather keep our clothes." .

"What's wrong with putting on a dress, my dear? You girls are much too pretty to be walking around here dressed in them black robes and men clothes like that. The church christening celebration is tonight. The whole town will be there! I got some real pretty outfits that just came in from New York City, come over here and let me show you. I see why you all caused such notice at the church site, looking at how young and pretty, you all are. Even that handsome boy, you all just look ... different ... *refined* I suppose is a good way to put it? And please, call me Mattie."

Angela replied, noticing Mattie pouting, "No disrespect to you or the dresses, Mattie."

At seeing Mattie's look of disappointment, Hope picked up one of the dresses.

"Mattie, on second thought, I'd like to try on a couple of these fancy New York dresses."

Delighted at the request, Mattie responded, "Oh my, yes ... please, be my guest!"

Angela, wearing a big smile, walked over to the woman and handed her the child.

"I would like very much to try on some also!"

"Of course you can, child!" Mattie's sparkling mood became infectious. She'd always dreamed of seeing her dresses modeled and the two young women were perfect.

"Mattie, these dresses are simply divine. Can we put on a real fashion show for you, accessories and all? It would be such a fun thing to do!"

"All'll rights! Now that is what I'm after! This is going to be such fun, and we are going to make a holiday show of it! Dressing rooms are over there, young ladies!" She clapped her hands together.

"Seth, you and the boys make way around the store to give the gals a promenade."

The men quickly cleared a path around the store while the women giggled and laughed like little girls playing dress up. Mattie motioned to Seth to get out his mouth organ. Pulling out his mouthpiece, he began playing a jazzy walking tune.

John stood up as the Master of Ceremonies.

"LADIES AND GENTLEMEN; this is what we have all been waiting for! We are honored to present Mademoiselle Mattie Stone's fashion collection, featuring this year's top runway models, ANGELA AND HOPE."

Seth started playing a funky mixture of way-down blues and Christmas carols. The gawking men stood mesmerized as the two beautiful girls-turned-models stepped out. They strutted and pranced, mugged and danced on their make-believe high fashion runway.

Shrilling with glee at having so much fun, the women eagerly matched and mixed outfits, putting a modern twist on them. With the accessories, they were giving Mattie fashion ideas she never would have imagined. Everyone was having so much fun laughing and joking. Mattie relished the moments.

The show over, Mattie sat with her eyes filled with tears of joy, happily clapping along with Easter sitting up in her lap. "I always dreamed of having a fashion show of my own with beautiful Negro models and just like that, you made it come to life. You both looked so pretty, I could not ask for more. Thank you both so much. You have given me such a wonderful Christmas gift! I feel like Jeremiah, now. You girls have made a dream of my own come true!"

While the women changed back into their clothes, Jerimiah was in heavy conversation with Seth, pointing at John's shoes. An old cobbler himself, Seth could not help but ask.

"Can I get a good look at those shoes you wearing, son?"

"Sure." John held one foot off the floor.

"I see the top of the shoe was made out of a very high quality white leather. Are they made of white buckskin or white buffalo hides?"

He rubbed his fingers against the raised Nike logo set on the ankle of the high-top shoe. He inspected the shoe again in admiration, amazed at the detailed, complicated construction and stitching. Seth walked behind John and lifted his foot, examining the bottom as though looking at a horse hoof.

"This sole isn't leather? What kind of material was this carved from, son?"

"It's called synthetic rubber," John answered.

"Sin … WHAT? Rubber? What's rubber? Where does that came from?' Seth questioned as he let go of John's leg.

"It comes from the sap of a tree," John answered.

"A rubber tree, you say?" Never having heard of such a thing, Seth realized he did not have the materials or tools to duplicate the shoe.

"They look like they could last for years, just what we Negros need around here. They look warm, too. How do they stand up to snow and water? I tell yam', if I could get some of those shoes here, I could … I mean *we* could make a fortune. How about sharing this with me? How I would get in touch with the fine cobbler that makes such a fantastic shoe, my friend? Maybe we can become partners?" Seth inquired.

John struggled through an explanation. "Well, that would be pretty difficult … they're kind of new, I guess you could say…. Mum, experimental … not out on the market yet. I'm kind of checking them out, breaking them in, so to speak."

"Oh, I see! Well you are going to draw a lot of attention parading around here wearing those white boots on your feet. Jerimiah already told me what happened when people at the church saw them."

"I think Uncle might have something you might be interested in! Ash hem!" Jerimiah suggested, nodding over to Seth.

Taking the cue, Seth scurried behind the counter, which was filled with boots. "Why don't you come over here, young man?"

John walked over to the boots on display.

"Go ahead and pick out anything you like for a trade."

Not seeing anything he liked in particular, John shook his head.

Seth frowned, then snapped his fingers. His face lit up and he grabbed a ladder from the other side of the store. He climbed up to the top shelf, reaching way in the back. He climbed back down, setting a big dusty black box on the counter. He blew the dust off the top of the box and paused. He slowly lifted off the lid. Seth's proud smile got even broader as he pulled out a beautiful pair of black snakeskin cowboy boots. The narrow, pointed boots were capped with silver tips, and a pair of silver spurs adorned the heels.

"Ooze, Unk, I didn't even know you had those or I'd be wearing them myself!" Jeremiah squawked out in jealously at seeing the shoes.

John grimaced imagining his toes scrunched up all day in the narrow boots. To everyone's disbelief, John shook his head, "No, thank you! I must say, those are some mighty fine kick-ass cowboy boots but, no thanks. I have this thing about snakes."

"No *thank* you?" Seth and Jeremiah replied in unison. Their smiles faded into the silence. Jeremiah's expression suddenly lit up, bringing back a big grin to his face.

"Hey, okay then, how about that cobbler my uncle was talking about? You can *hook* us up to the man, right, my brother?" he asked John.

"Hook us up to what?" Seth asked.

"Hook us up with the cobbler, Unk!" Jeremiah explained, nudging his elbow into Seth's ribs. Seth scratched his head, looked quizzical for a moment. Then, getting it, he repeated the Ebonics phrase loudly. "Oh yeah, I get it! Hook us up son, with the, Man…. The *man*ufacturer, that is!" Seth added a little of his own flavor to the slang. Everyone in the store cracked up.

A sudden pounding on the front door brought the laughter to an abrupt halt. An angry loud voice shouted from outside.

"It's me, the sheriff—open up this door, Seth. I know you got them strangers in there!"

Chapter 12

"So We Meet Again!"

"It's the sheriff! I shore hope you all don't have no troubles with him—he can be a mean old pole cat!" Seth warned. He walked over to look out the door from behind the pulled shade. Seeing Seth peep out, the callous Sheriff banged his fist against the window in Seth's face.

"Seth! Open this damn door, I'm not going to say it again, boy!"

Seth jumped and unlocked the door, fumbling. It swung open, and in walked the sheriff, Ezekiel Joppa. The bell above the door clanged radically, almost breaking off its hook.

Even though he is now a Caucasian, immediately she recognized the fugitive. Angela flashed back to Ezekiel Joppa sitting in the back of her patrol car, stone drunk with his crooked smile, and then mysteriously escaping her custody.

*Yes, it's the same man, all right, and now he's back here …
the County Sheriff of Mariah? That makes two men from my
future I have to deal with here in the past.*

Meanwhile, not as clear about him as she, John was
having a battle with his memory as to why this man's
face was so menacingly familiar. *Where have I seen this
man before?*

Two big, raunchy deputies with shotguns crashed
through the back door. Ezekiel chomped on a big cigar
butt, steadily keeping his one eye trained on Angela. He
slowly walked toward her when his attention was caught
by the pair of fancy black cowboy boots Seth had left
displayed on the counter.

"Weee doggie, Seth! I've been looking all over this
county for a pair of boots just like these. Why looky here,
they even come outfitted with silver tips covering the toe
and sharp heavy spurs attached! You mind if I try them
on, Seth?" he asked, already peeling off his old boots.

Seth responded with a regretful tone, "Yeah, no, no …
I mean, yes, go right ahead, Sheriff, try them on! They
look like they might be a little small to me."

Seth prayed the sheriff's feet were too large.

"I'll sell them to you for half price—twenty dollars for
this forty-dollar pair of boots." Seth offered, overcharging
him for the twelve-dollar boots. Ezekiel gave him a look
that said "you can't be serious." He sat down on the sacks
of flour and easily put on the fancy black boots. The
sheriff stood up and walked around, constantly looking
over at the three odd strangers, rubbing on his long beard.

"A perfect fit ... put 'em on my tab, Seth!" Seth's face turned sour.

"You mean on top of the fifty dollars you already owe me, Sheriff?" he asked, mad at himself for leaving the shoes out in the first place.

Jeremiah sighed and slumped his shoulders, shaking his head in disappointment at having no chance at the snazzy boots now.

The sheriff smirked.

"Why are you looking like that, Jeremiah? You worried about me not making good on my debt?" He turned to Seth.

"Who knows, Seth? With me in your debt you may need a favor from me one day!"

"No, no—I know you're good for it, Sheriff," Seth submissively lied as the intimidating sheriff stood over him.

"Anything else I can help you with, Sheriff?" Seth patronized him with a nervous smile.

"Nope, I'm done with you! Just keep quiet while I ask these ... ah, *new folks* here a few questions." He turned and points to each of the three newcomers, and then to the now-wailing child.

"We've been on the lookout for some murdering Negros not from around these parts carting around a stolen black newborn baby! They killed and butchered the mother, taking the child right from her womb."

Angela looked over to Jeremiah.

The Sheriff became livid at the child's loud wailings. He threw his old boots to his deputy, Charlie. He covered one ear and pointed the cigar butt in his other hand at the baby.

"Somebody better hurry up and shut that little monkey up!" he yelled out in anger.

"It's a baby. Crying is what they do!" John defiantly responded with attitude, immediately sparking up trouble. The child continued to scream at the top of her lungs.

The sheriff turned swiftly and confronted him, his good eye looking at John, all crazy.

"Hey! Ain't nobody talking to you!" He angrily sized up John. "Who you think you talking to, boy?" He turned to his two deputies. "Was I talking to him, fellas?"

"No, Sheriff!" a smirking deputy answered.

"Nope, sure wasn't!" the other said, sneering.

John foolishly took a step forward. In a blink, the sheriff pulled his gun out.

"Take another step, ya' hear, and I will blow your face off. Where you from, boy, and what business brings you here to my county?" The big man glared his one eye at John.

Uncle Seth stepped between John and the sheriff.

"The boy don't mean no harm to you, Sheriff, he's a newcomer to these parts." He sheepishly points to the back of the store. "And your fella's didn't have to go busting down my back door like that, Sheriff Joppa. Now I'm going to have to fix it before I can close up today," Seth whined, complaining.

"Hey! You think I care about busting down your damn back door? I'm the law round these parts and you got possible dangerous suspects hiding up in here!" So irritated having to speak over the crying child, he warned for the last time, pointing his gun at the baby.

"You all better shut that baby up pretty quick or I'm going to stuff a handkerchief down its throat."

Angela lifted the child from Mattie's arms and whispered into her ear. The baby stopped crying immediately. She handed the baby back to Mattie.

"What is it that you want with us, Sheriff?" Angela asked.

"Don't play dumb with me! You heard me the first time! We are looking for a stolen newborn child kidnapped and traveling with three wicked, murdering Negros that practice black magic!"

He turned to Mattie. "And it looks like you've been hiding them right here in your store, Mattie. I bet this is the baby and these are the three murdering culprits I'm looking for!" He pointed, jutting his cigar butt at the newcomers.

Mattie provided an excellent alibi for her new friends in a desperate attempt to protect them. "First of all, this child is not no new born baby, Sheriff! Look at her!" Mattie held the big baby up for the sheriff to see. The sheriff sees the baby is obviously not a newborn child. Mattie pointed to Angela.

"Angela here is my sister's friend's daughter; she travels with her friends, John and Hope, this child is theirs. Hearing about our progress here, they have just arrived in time to celebrate the holidays with us and are thinking about moving to Mariah.

"There are no stolen newborn babies around here! Stolen from where and from whom? You know us, Sheriff, and we would not allow no black magic voodoo people in my store! We are good Christians, me and Seth and Jeremiah. We are not the kind to befriend or welcome some voodoo worshippers or black magic in our place, no, Lordy!"

The sheriff gave her a disrespectful smirk and turned to Angela. Waving his pistol at her, he barked, "You there, the one with the funny colored hair, get over here!" He squinted at her with his one good eye, observing her colorful braids. He watched carefully as Angela slowly walked up and stopped in front of him. The sheriff beamed a warped smile.

Seeing his crooked grin, John remembered how he knew this man. He took an aggressive step, but out the corner of his eye, the big Sheriff caught his movement.

Before anyone could react, something spectacular occurred. Angela stepped in and waved her hand between the sheriff's gun and John. A blue aura appeared, freezing everyone in place except Hope. Immediately on the attack, Hope moved with phenomenal speed, snatching the shotgun out of the motionless deputy's hands and knocking him unconscious. She moved Mattie and the child out of harm's way. She flew in front of the other deputy and whacks him in the face with the gun. She then tossed the weapon on the floor.

The now wide-awake sheriff stood, still frozen stiff, in front of Angela. His one good eye frantically followed her as she slowly walks around him. He was angry as hell as Angela calmly spoke to him.

"Remember me and the two dead friends you left in Mariah in the burned up SUV?"

He glared with hatred at her. Each time she passed by the gun barrel, he desperately tried but was unable to pull the trigger.

"Remember telling me, 'I ain't going to need no lawyer and I ain't going to jail' while you sat in the back of my squad car, giggling like a little girl?" Angela mimicked the sheriff, adding a low growl.

The hard expression on his evil, squinting face changed into one of outrageous recognition. The sheriff laughed in her face, especially amused by the growl.

"Oh, yeah, I remember you and your crybaby friend over there, now ... *Sheriff*!

Angela stopped walking. "Ohhh—I see you recognize me."

"I told you we would meet again, didn't I? You sure you know what you are dealing with coming here? 'Cause you all just crossed the line showing up back here my town. His bent nose twitched. And this weak spell you got me under? When it does pass, I am going to catch up with you and personally burn your black ass, witch." His nose twitched again.

She looked at Sheriff Joppa with aversion and disdain, then answered his challenge.

"Why play this game? I know who you are and you know who we are. Even the child could smell your foul evil presence before you walked through these good people's door." With that, she unleashed a powerful knee kick right between his legs. She delivered another sidewinding kick to his face, breaking his twitching nose. The force of the kick knocked him out and onto the floor. He slumped down, out cold, his nose knocked out of place and bleeding profusely.

"Now *that* was how you looked when we first met!"

The store became suddenly silent and still as the three Moloch lay unconscious on the floor. Hope released Seth and Mattie. They stood witness to everything that occurred.

Angela turned to Mattie, taking the child out of her arms.

"I am so sorry for all this and bringing these evil men into your store! Please forgive us, but we must leave here right now!"

Fearful and confused, Mattie pled to Angela.

"Wait, please, I got to know! What the sheriff said about you all stealing the baby and worshipping black magic, please tell me this is not true?"

"Yes, tell us." Seth said, backing his wife. "We don't want to have no trouble with you or the law.

"We saw and heard everything that just happened.

We do not have *anything* to do with no evil black magic here. Was it black magic you just used on the sheriff? *Have* you done what he accuses? What Mattie said to the sheriff is true. We are good Christian people. We don't hold with breaking the law, and we don't need no trouble with that sheriff. He is as mean a red neck as they come. You need to tell us just what in God's name is going on.."

Angela explained gently, "We protect the child from the likes him and those like him. He is a Moloch."

"Okay … I don't love the sheriff none, and he might well be a mollusk or whatever you claim, but I didn't see no blue flashes coming out *his* hands!"

Hope tried to help calm their nerves and erase any doubts they were having. "This is the Lord's work that you stand witness to, not any black magic. We work in His name to thwart the evil of the Moloch. The sheriff is pure evil, and he has not shown his powers, which are formidable."

"Then we are surely placed in jeopardy, I fear, as my wife does!"

Mattie turned to Angela and asked in a low voice, "So you really are the angel … the one my boy always talks about … the one in his dreams?" She nodded toward Jeremiah, who stood near John at the front of the store, still under the spell.

Angela took Mattie and Seth's hands into her own.

"Yes, we do know each other, he speaks the truth…. However, what he doesn't know is I share the same dreams of him! Look at us, and you will see we are not part of any evil conspiracy as Joppa accuses. He is the true evil here. He is the deceiver and is more evil that you can ever imagine!"

The married couple stood witness as a pale blue aura covered Hope and Angela to unveil their true form. They stood together in majestic splendor, fitted in full battle dress of golden armor. A beautiful revelation to behold, Seth praised what he saw before him.

"Lord Jesus, Mattie. Tis true what she speaks! Jeremiah's dreams were true."

Mattie concurred by bowing her head, placing one hand on her heart and one raised high.

"Glory is the beauty of them! Yes, tis true, Seth, tis true! Thank you, Lord!"

"Thank you for lifting the veil and opening our eyes to the truth!" Seth humbly cried out.

Angela spoke. "We must leave now!"

Mattie, with tears in her eyes, gave them her blessings. Taking hold of Seth's hand, she whispered to Angela.

"Thank you so much, my charming child, for making this my merriest Christmas. Most of all for being real and not just a dream trapped inside my boy's head. Do what you must to protect yourselves and the child. Thank you for giving me my fashion show and making a dream of my own come true. I understand my calling, now! I no longer hold fear of what to expect from this world—you've shown me what waits for me after!" She kissed Angela lovingly on the forehead.

"You take good care of my boy, you hear? We will meet up with you all at the church celebration. We got a lot to celebrate tonight! I can't wait to tell Reverend Bishop about all this!"

Hope turned and waved her hand toward John, bringing him out of his trance. Becoming conscious, John finished his attempt to attack, swinging at nothing in the air where Sheriff Joppa had stood moments before. He looked around in a daze and saw the sheriff lying on the floor near him, out cold. Blood was flowing over his beard from his broken nose.

"What happened? Did I do that?" He proudly rubbed his balled-up right fist.

Hope looked sarcastically at Angela then back to John, and released Jeremiah out of his suspended state.

Jeremiah, dismayed and torn seeing the sheriff sprawled out on the floor, wondered what had been going on.

"Jeremiah, John, come, we must take care of these bodies and leave here as soon as possible!" Hope appealed to the men.

Jeremiah was not privy to the revelation his aunt and uncle received and still questioned if the three were evil, as the Sheriff said before he blacked out. Very concerned regarding the safety of his family, he was certain about one thing; when the sheriff came back around, he would surely seek revenge on all of them.

CHAPTER 13

Challenges

aybe now is the time to take my leave of them. Jeremiah silently deliberated before posing his questions to the travelers.

"What about my uncle and aunt—you plan on leaving them here alone? How will they avoid the sheriff's scorn? Maybe it is best I stay here with them." Hope tried to allay Jeremiah's fears.

"I promise, they will be safe; the sheriff and his men will not be here when they awake. Seth and Mattie will not remember anything that has taken place and neither will they."

Hope gave the child to Angela and walked over to Seth and Mattie. She sat them down and quietly whispered to the couple. They closed their eyes and fell fast asleep. Her hands glowed as she placed one on each of their foreheads.

"We will meet with you at the church. Should the sheriff cross your path you with tell him the truth, you will only have memories of our arrival. Inform him that the newcomers came, passing through town with a child, and left." She turned to Jeremiah. "They will be protected now! They will follow when they awake, however we must get rid of the sheriff and his men and leave here now!"

John and Jeremiah moved the three unconscious men next to the busted door in the rear of the store. Jeremiah told the others of his plan.

"I'll go fetch their horses from the front of the store and pretend like I'm taking them down to the livery stable at the other end of town. I am going to circle round back behind the store. Once I fix the door, we can leave."

Rushing out of the store, it still troubled him to leave Seth and Mattie behind. He grabbed the reins of the horses and mounted Maribel, running his hand over the covered weapons strapped to the side, making sure they were still there.

Meanwhile, back inside the store, John snatched up the double-barreled shotgun and held it to the back of the unconscious sheriff's head. Hope shouted at him in horror.

"John, stop, what are you doing?"

"I'm going to blow his freaking head off, Hope…. He's the man that killed my parents and he ain't disappearing on me this time!" Filled with hate, John shoved the shotgun barrel harder against the sheriff's head.

"No, John, you cannot! That is not our way!" Hope pleaded, and Angela coldly warned him.

"You dare consider the worst sin of all! Committing murder of one who cannot defend himself? It will not do!

Such an act may jeopardize everything and you know I can't allow that to happen, John!"

"How can *you* say that, Angela? You were there when it all happened! You saw what he did to my parents! He is not going to pull one of those disappearing acts on us this time and get away! We have the chance to rid ourselves of him now!" Tension rose as they stared at one another. "We never proved any of that John."

"So what are you going to do if I do him, kill me, Angela? I don't care, because I'm taking out my revenge! I will gladly give my life to take my vengeance upon this man! If I kill him now, here in the past, it might change things in the future— it might even bring back my mom and dad!"

Hope was terribly upset hearing hotheaded John's wicked remarks.

"I cannot believe this blasphemy! You speak of raising the dead. Killing him will not bring them back, John! What has happen has happened! It is what it is! What is with you? 'Revenge is mine,' saith the Lord! You cannot commit cold-blooded murder like this. Why do you stray like this, John? Joppa is a Moloch, a powerful, evil paranormal being. He has the power to travel through time. He takes control of weak minds and souls in order to kill and disrupt. Listen to me, the sheriff's departure from this world approaches soon, John. All will be put right. Have faith."

"Oh, yeah, well, you're right about that, he is getting ready to depart from here, all right. Dis part of his head is going over there; another piece is going to depart that way and another part—"

"Stop it, John! Put the gun down at once! This sinful act will change everything and I told you, John, I am not allowing that to happen."

Intimidated by her threats, John hesitated. Hope took the opportunity to snatch the shotgun from John, running for the door.

Angry and belligerent, John caught her and snatched the gun back. He walked back and placed the barrel of the gun against the head of the unconscious sheriff.

"What is it that you all don't get?" He cocks both triggers. "Why are you both against me on this? This ... whatever he is, murdered my mother and father! He killed that child's mother! I will have my revenge! "

"Please, John, no! Please, please, do not pull that trigg—!" John squeezed both triggers before she could finish her plea.

"CLICK, CLICK!"

Everyone was astounded when no shotgun blast occurred.

Angela let out a huge sigh of relief. "Thank you!"

John opened the chamber to find both barrels empty. He scowled at Hope with angry eyes. She stared back at him, profoundly saddened. She slowly raised and opened her closed hand to reveal the two missing shotgun shells.

"You should have forgiven, not try to reap vengeance."

Not saying a word, John snatched the bullets out of her hand and ran out the back of the store.

"John, come back!" Hope shouted after him. She turned her tearful gaze to Angela, then over to the helpless Sheriff Joppa, still out cold on the floor. She and Angela have recognized that John has failed his challenge miserably. Sadly, she repeated her earlier statement.

"Yes, John. His time to leave here approaches, and so does yours, my brother . . . so does yours. You should have forgiven."

We have already been compromised by John's actions, Hope!" Angela warned, taking command. "We must return to the church for sanctuary now, with no delay. It is the only safe place that evil cannot breach unless invited. We must get ready and be prepared, for when the sheriff awakes, our battle surely begins."

As though she hadn't heard, Hope said, "He has to find his true self and ask to be forgiven for all he has done before he runs out of time."

Angela sympathized. "It is his own free will with which he makes his choices, Hope. You know I can feel how much you still love him. You cannot hide the feelings from me, as hard as you have tried. I, too, have love in my heart for that man, Jeremiah, but these men cannot come before what we have to do here is completed, Hope!"

"I know . . . I know all too well!" Hope sadly whispered. They hugged one another tightly.

* * *

Angry and tormented, John stopped running at the end of the alley. Turning to look back down to the store, he reloaded the gun. He considered going back to finish the job of blowing the sheriff's brains out when Jeremiah turned the corner, riding into the alley. Jeremiah started at seeing John standing in front of him, loading the shotgun. John's mind was still set on killing the sheriff, and he grabbed hold of an idea. Bluntly, he made his intentions known.

"I want that sheriff . . . I want to see him dead. What do you think about that?"

"You are not alone, my brother. He is hated by many in these parts and you can count on the fact that he is going to kill all of you should he remember any of this," Jeremiah answered.

"And you, also, if he catches you with us— and your aunt and uncle too ... that is, if we let him!" John insinuated his intent. Seeing the look of concern on Jeremiah's face, John made the proposition.

"We need to rid ourselves of any more threats from him."

"Let me whittle on that proposition a bit. Come on, let's go straighten out this mess inside and get out of here before something else happens," Jeremiah answered, looking down at John's shoes.

I sure hope Seth and Mattie are out of harm's way, and I know one thing, nothing better happen to them!

Chapter 14

Till Death Do Us Part

Jeremiah felt the tension rise in the air immediately when they walked back into the rear of the store. Jeremiah noticed that Angela was extremely distraught. She glared at John disdainfully, seeing that he still had possession of the shotgun.

"What's going on?" he asked. No one spoke a word.

Hope shamefully turned and wiped her tears away. Jeremiah, bothered by the uncomfortable silence, turned to John.

"They are upset because I wanted to kill the sheriff."

Jeremiah frowned. "Come on ... let's get these boys out of here so we can head back to the church."

They securely tied the three unconscious men on their horses. Hope whispered into the ear of each horse. She stepped back and said, "Not too fast, now! Giddyap!"

The horses trotted off into the woods.

"Jeremiah, we must seek sanctuary before dark," Hope explained.

"We are going back to the church to see Reverend Bishop! He will help us." Jeremiah and John quickly boarded up the back door. The group left town unseen through the woods to seek sanctuary at the Church of God.

Meanwhile, in the alley, back behind the general store, a large empty wooden crate barrel stirred. A boy named Anthony climbed out, having hidden inside. He was in the alley the whole time, eating a candy cane in peace before taking home the groceries he had purchased from the store just before the newcomers' arrival. When the deputies rode up in the alley, to avoid trouble, he'd hidden inside the barrel. Hearing the deputies bum rush the back door, he peeked through the slats in the crate to get a look at what was going on inside. Anthony heard everything about the stolen baby and evil black voodoo witches. Straining to see, he'd stuck another big piece of candy cane in his mouth to watch the action.

Quietly climbing out, he'd peeked inside just in time to catch Angela glow a bright pale blue, knocking the sheriff out cold. Then he saw Hope moving in a blazing speed, taking out the deputies. Gasping in shock, he began choking on the large piece of candy caught in his throat. He covered his mouth to muffle the choking sound as he coughed up the chunk of peppermint. When the ruckus died down, he looked back inside the store, catching the rest of what happened.

Wide eyed and unseen, he watched John burst out the back door, running down the alley in those fancy white shoes. He waited silently as Jeremiah and John returned.

He peeped at the newcomers, the pretty witch with the golden hair cast more spells, talking to the sheriffs' horses, sending them trotting into the woods with the sheriff and his men tied to their backs. Carefully, he listened to Jeremiah talking about going and hiding out at the new church.

He remained hidden for a while, making sure everyone had left. After what he had just witnessed, he was convinced of the sheriff's allegations about the strangers. He decided he could get the groceries home later, if he brought home some extra cash to make up for the delay.

His mouth watered as he thought of the reward he would get. Maybe he could get a nickel, or a dime, maybe as much as a silver dollar! Then the white shoes flashed in his mind. As he pretended he was running in the white shoes the newcomer wore, the damp cold air streaming over his hot face was exhilarating. He ran faster through the woods, deeply breathing in the brisk cold air of the winter's afternoon.

To him, the white shoes by far were a fair deal for all the information he had to give to the sheriff. He was going to make a killing off this, and possibly reap a big cash reward on top of it all.

Meanwhile, deep in the woods, down on the ground, his face in a cold pool of his own blood, Ezekiel Joppa regained consciousness, dumbfounded. His head was throbbing as he looked at his horse grazing nearby. He could not understand the pain from his throbbing nose or the fall from off his horse that had woken him from the nothingness. Even still, he was steaming mad and in a lot of pain.

He looked around for his two deputies. Charlie lay on the ground near him. He opened his eyes, staring blankly at the sheriff.

"Owwwl! What happened?" he asked, confused and lost.

The sheriff rubbed a huge knot on the back of his head, trying to think.

They both looked over just in time to see Macklin slide off the side his horse, landing with a heavy thud, flat on his face.

Charlie rubbed his swollen mouth. Macklin came to. He grimaced in pain, grabbing his swollen jaw. He then moaned even more, touching his swollen brow and black eye.

Macklin looked over to the others and asked, "How the heck did we get here? The last thing I remember we was riding up toward town."

Ezekiel sat on the ground, confounded, his mind blank and his nose broken. Most importantly, he could not remember when, why or who had kicked their asses. He could not account for the time lost or how they got to the place where they were. He straightened out his crooked nose with a crack, howling in pain like a wounded animal. He got up off the ground.

"What happened to us, boss?" Macklin asked again, still rubbing head.

Sheriff Joppa frowned over at his baffled deputies and said nothing, not knowing himself what had taken place. He retrieved his horse.

He placed his foot in the stirrup and stared at the beautiful new black cowboy boot all decked out with silver spurs and silver tips at the toe. The longer he looked at the boot in the stirrup, the more his face began to scowl. Even though his nose was broken and clogged with blood, he sniffed the air and caught the lingering scent of the child, Easter. He looked up at the sun sitting low in the sky and figured that more than just a few minutes had passed. It had been hours. He then shouted, "We've been bamboozled.... Saddle up!" He mounted and turned his horse around, galloping back toward town.

"Bam *what*?" The fat deputy asked, rushing to get back on his horse.

"Boozled!" Macklin, already mounted, repeated.

"We done went and got ourselves damn hoodwinked!"

"Hood *what*?" The fat man asked.

The sheriff shook his head wearily at the two fools riding up next to him. He dug his new silver-spiked spurs deep into his horse's ribs. The horse reared up, then took off in a frantic gallop toward town. Whipping his horse violently, he shouted back to his men in anger.

"Follow me! We going back to the general store!"

* * *

A horse and buggy stood outside the general store. The bell over the door chimed softly as the elderly couple stepped outside. A cold, thick fog slowly rolled in and engulfed the town.

"Will you looky there! Where did all this strange fog come from? Hurry up, Seth, we're late! You know we supposed to done meet Jeremiah and the others with that cute little baby at the church. I do not understand how we just fell asleep like that! We should have been at the celebration hours ago!" Mattie complained.

Seth had changed into a new pair of overalls and a new burgundy cotton shirt and overcoat. Mattie had already put it together to match her swank burgundy outfit.

"My Lord, it's cold out here, and now we have to deal with this dang old fog!" Seth locked up while Mattie complained, tying her stylish matching bonnet. He buttoned his shirt collar, looking worriedly at the thickening mist. "I guess we were more tired than we thought doing all that restocking of supplies and inventory work without Jeremiah's help. I can't believe that boy showed up so late with them newcomers and that pretty lil' baby they carried with them."

"Let's just thank the Lord it wasn't his baby he brought home with him!" Mattie shuddered as the cold evening wind blew by.

"I need my wrap, Seth, and you better grab a scarf yourself!"

They both returned inside the store. Coming back outside with their winter woolens, they were locking up again as the sheriff and his two deputies rode out of the fog, stopping in front of their store.

Shocked, Seth nervously greeted them.

"Hello, Sheriff, we were just closing up! Can we help you with something?"

Ezekiel spoke to them through the handkerchief he held to his nose.

"You know why I'm here, Seth. I am searching for a black female newborn baby. She travels with three Negro strangers, two colored women and a colored boy that stole her!" The sheriff wiped at his still dripping nose. Ezekiel paused to spit blood out of his mouth. Before they could answer, his eye glared, full of fury, and he gave warning, "I already know that they have passed this way and been in your store. So don't try to lie to me!"

Mattie stepped back into her husband's arms, intimidated by the bleeding man.

"Yes, sir, there were three visitors here with a female child, but the baby didn't look like no newborn to me. The child was at the least six months."

"Did they tell you where they were from or where they journey to?" the sheriff questioned further.

"They were just passing through to barter goods. We gave them some goat's milk for the child and they continued on their way. We cannot say in which direction they left, Sheriff, 'cause we don't know." Seth honestly replied.

"You sure there weren't four that traveled together with the child, Mattie?" The crafty sheriff asked, directing his question to the frightened woman. Understanding his intent, Mattie did not respond and tried to hide her worry for Jeremiah's safety.

"Don't stand there looking stupid making me wait for your answer, Mattie! So where is your boy, Jeremiah?

"We have no reason to lie to you," Mattie responded timidly.

"The newcomers that were here seem like three right friendly strangers to me, Sheriff. Just like Seth said, they stopped by and they asked if we had some milk or water for the baby. I gave them some. The child was no newborn, Sheriff, she was a big baby!"

"You old fools! These young evil pretenders have tricked you. The child is in great danger. Do not try to protect them. Tell me what I need to know and I might consider being lenient on the both of you. The ones who have the baby in their possession stole the child. They killed the mother, cutting the child right out of her womb. The strangers you met today possess evil black magic. They are what you people call voodoo worshippers. They wish to feed on the child's blood then sacrifice her heart to their black magic idol! Mattie, I want you to tell me which direction your boy and them witches headed in."

She looked in the direction of the church before she closed her eyes, shaking her head. "We cannot help you, Sheriff," she answered.

"Sorry, Sheriff. We can't tell you what we do not know!" Seth defiantly replied, stepping up.

The sheriff looked down at Mattie from atop his horse. "So where is that big Negro of yours? Where is he, Mattie?"

His anger grew by the second at their silent misdirection. His urge is to smite them right where they stood. Instead, in a calm voice, the Sheriff asked Mattie again. "Where did the evil ones take your boy, Mattie? Where are these pretenders? They might have him under their spell."

Mattie's voice shook, responding, "I told you, I don't know. We both just woke up from a nap, Sheriff, not more than an hour ago. I have not seen Jeremiah since this afternoon. We have no idea what direction the strangers headed in when they left. We would tell you if we knew and that's the honest to God's truth, Sheriff!"

"I'm not fooling with you two, you best be telling me the truth."

Seth stepped forward, noticing the Sheriff wearing the fancy new black boots. He shouted, "Oh, yeah, by the way, Sheriff, don't forget you owe me twenty dollars for those boots."

"Seth, when did I come by and buy these boots from you?"

Seth did not respond. Mattie and he suddenly and clearly remembered the sheriff coming into their store earlier and all that had occurred after.

Unfortunately, so did the evil sheriff, and his rage exploded like a volcano. He pulled his hat down low, then popped his coat collar up. He turned his horse back around to face the couple. He roared, "Hey, boy, answer my question! When was I here?"

They stood in terror as howling winds grew louder and began to swirl the fog around the store. Joppa addressed his deputies, hiding his face.

"I want you boys to watch this. Best you move back a ways."

Ghastly shadows appear in the swirling fog. Mattie nudged up closer behind Seth as the fog began to move in on them. The sheriff lifted up his head and revealed his true self. Mattie screamed in terror at the sight of his heinous face. He chanted a spell and waved his arm. The store erupted into a flaming inferno. Mattie turned and screamed in anguish.

"Seth! The store, it's on fire, he's burning our store!" Seth fumbled with the keys, trying to open the door. The bell clanged loudly as he managed to swing it open. A giant snake of swirling flames burning inside turned its fiery head to the door.

"Oh, my God, Seth! What in the name of Jesu...?" Mattie buried her face into her husband's chest as the flaming snake lashed out, swallowing them. A ball of fire shot out of its mouth, hurling out the front door. It landed, burning in the street in front of the sheriff's horse. The head of the giant flaming snake looked out the door, searching around, then slithered back into finish its evil work of destroying the store. The sizzling ball turned into ash and blew away in the howling winds.

The deputies sat, petrified and wide-eyed, looking on in frightful bewilderment.

"Weeeeeee doggie! Did ya see that?" Charlie shouted, slapping his thigh in amusement at the spectacle.

"Yeah, I did!" Macklin shouted back, showing a mouth of missing teeth.

They turned to the sheriff, his back still turned, hiding his demon form.

"Where is she? How did that old fool Mattie escape my wrath?" He disappeared, howling into the fog on the hunt after her.

The crisp winter air hung heavy with the wet, smoldering smell of sulfuric ash and water. A huge, ominous black cloud of smoke hovered over the town as the sun began to set. Finding only the remains of Seth people searched unsuccessfully for his wife. Trampled in the middle of the muddy street, the only thing found of her was a scorched new burgundy-and-white shawl. It was as if Mattie Stone had disappeared off the face of the earth.

CHAPTER 15

A Penny for Your Thoughts

The young boy, Anthony, sat on a tree stump, exhausted from running through the woods in search of the sheriff. A chill came over him and, to his terrifying amazement, a fog bank suddenly appeared in front of him. The sheriff and the deputies rode out of it to stop right in front him. The frightened boy did not hesitate to start telling what he knew.

"Hey, Sheriff, I been looking all over for you. Are you still looking for those three strangers with that baby who jumped you at the general store earlier? 'Cause I gots a lots of information for you."

"You mean those ruthless, cutthroat, demon-worshipping Negros I'm chasing that just killed Seth and Mattie Stone?" The sheriff responded.

The boy reeled back in shock from the news. "Seth and Mattie are dead?"

"Yep, they have been murdered, set on fire alive and burnt, right in their store! Both are deader than a doornail killed by them evil colored newcomers! We are tracking them now. So what you got, boy? And you better not be wasting my time."

"Is there a reward for information, Sheriff?" the boy nervously asked.

"Why shore, there is always a big reward for capturing murderers and kidnappers, son!" Laughing, the sheriff and the deputies dismounted their horses and surrounded the boy. "That is, if you got something that's helping me capture them. He tossed the boy a coin.

"What I got is worth a lot more than a penny, Sheriff."

The boy's attempt to negotiate a deal irritated Ezekiel to no end. "*What's been getting in to you Negros round here all of a sudden?* got to hear what you got first, boy," he said, growling in anger.

Charlie laughed and snorted, "I see we got us another one dem smart-ass niggar boys here, Charlie, a real bizznessman! See! I warned ya! Ever since Lincoln freed our doggone slaves, they've all sudden done went and got smart and sassy on us po' old country white boys!"

"You all just stop scaring the boy like that! I think this boy can help us in more ways than we think." The sheriff winked and nodded to his men.

"Sheriff, I didn't mean no disrespect to your offer, but I think what I gots to tell is at least worth them shoes the newcomer boy you tracking is wearing!" Anthony lifted up his feet to show the sheriff a big hole on the soles of both his shoes. To Anthony's surprise, the sheriff reached into his vest and handed the boy a twenty-five cent piece.

"Well, now, let's see here, I tell you what, if you got something good to tell me and help in catching those murdering black scoundrels, you can keep the money *and* have the boy's shoes. Besides, when I catch that boy, he ain't going to need no shoes hanging from a rope no ways, huh, boys?" He started laughing, turning to his deputies. "Ha, ha, ha oww, damn that hurts!" he loudly complained, squinting in pain and covering his nose with his handkerchief.

Deputy Macklin joined in on the taunts.

"Yeah, he sure ain't going to need no shoes ... after we burn his black ass with them other heathen Negro witches!" .

"Yeah, I can't wait to see that damn Jeremiah burn for being in cahoots with them witches and anybody else that's helping them with their getaway. He *was* with them, right?" The sheriff asked the boy.

A big grin spread across the young boy's face.

"Yep, he sure was, and I saw them strangers use their blue glowing witchcraft on you and the deputies to get the jump on you. Heck and that ain't all! When she knocked you out, the new boy tried to blow your head off with a shotgun, Sheriff! You sure were lucky them chamber barrels were empty. I heard them talking to Jeremiah about where he was taking them to hide out and be safe!"

"You saw all this and you know where they were headed?" The sheriff grabbed hold of Anthony and glared a grim evil look at the boy.

"Yup!" the frightened boy eagerly responded.

"And you will testify that Jeremiah was in co-hoots with them if they make it to trial?"

With no hesitation, the boy nodded.

"Yes, sir. He was in with them, all right. I ain't got no problem testifying and swearing to the truth about what I seen with my own eyes and what I heard them say with my own ears!"

"Well, now, I see we got us a right smart star witness here, boys! He's just chock full of information that's going to come in right handy at trial!" He tossed the boy another penny.

"I heard one of those women talking about getting to a holy saint . . . u . . . something? Jeremiah was taking them over to Reverend Bishop's new church for protection. It's being built not that far from here."

"And you are going to volunteer to show us where that church is, ain't ya boy? And point out those murderers!" the sheriff commanded.

"I sure would like to, Sheriff, but my momma's been waiting on me to bring back these groceries for dinner that I got at the store right before them strangers came in." He pointed to the burlap sack on the ground. He badly wanted to leave. "I'm sorry, but I got to get back home. Look here, I can draw you a map." He picked up a stick and started drawing on the ground. Kicking the stick out of the boy's hand, the sheriff asked, "You want those shoes and that reward, doesn't you, boy?"

"Yes, sir, I do. But I's best be getting home, sir!" His eyes looked nervously back toward town to see the black smoke rising.

The sheriff nodded at Macklin, who slapped his shotgun butt against the boy's head, knocking him down to the ground. The other deputy pulled the boy by his jacket collar, forcibly lifting him off the ground. The other deputy walked over with two bullwhips in his hand.

Sheriff Joppa looked on, smiling as they unmercifully whipped the screaming boy. He plotted a deceiving scheme in which the boy would play an important part.

"I will give you a reward of ten silver dollars and the boy's shoes you spoke of if you become part of my posse and help us capture them."

Anthony, not having much choice, agrees to join in the hunt. He would be the perfect pawn that will help with the capture of the newcomers and the child the sheriff desperately sought.

CHAPTER 16

Broken Spells and Broken Promises

Jeremiah hurried the travelers through the woods. John lagged behind in troubled silence, his attempted murder of the Sheriff failed. He had yet to speak to either Hope or Angela since the incident in the store. As the sun sank below the trees, Jeremiah walked down the wooded path ahead of the strangers. Hope was leading the horse, walking beside Angela, who sat in somber silence atop Jeremiah's horse. She lovingly held the child, Easter, close to her body, keeping her warm.

Hope and Angela caught the faintest foul stench of sulfur before it evaporated into the crisp, cold air. Their senses heightened. Hope looked, concerned, back in the direction of Mariah. She was anxious seeing the black cloud hovering above the town against the dimming sky.

Angela received word from above of Jeremiah's aunt and uncle's tragedy, and she began to cry silently, mourning. Knowing her spell on the sheriff was now broken, she also knew he would soon come after them. She turned to Hope with an expression of despair covering her beautiful face. She felt behind the saddle to make sure their weapons were within reach.

"Our weapons are gone!" Angela whispered to Hope, shocked at finding their golden swords were missing.

"No, they're not, I got you! I have our weapons safely hidden here under my robe." She revealed their blades. "I wanted them close. You had better watch that man of yours, girl, because I will kill him should he become a threat when you tell him of what has happened."

"And the same goes for John should he fail in what has to be done." Angela cautioned. "I must inform Jeremiah of his aunt and uncle's passing." Deep in sorrow, she somberly calls out to him. "Jeremiah, we need to stop. I must speak with you for a minute."

"Yes, of course, my angel," Jeremiah cheerfully responded. Angela dismounted, handing the child to Hope. Hope turned to John, walking up the trail from behind. She spoke to him for the first time since the incident. "Angela and Jeremiah need some privacy. Come, John, you and I need to talk." She turned first to Angela and Jeremiah. "We must get the child to the church before nightfall. Check behind us and cover our trail, we want to be sure no one is following us."

"Got it!" Jeremiah responded, pulling up brush and wiping away the trail left behind. Angela walked over to John and grabbed a tight hold to the back of his neck. Drawing him to her, she placed her face flush against his cheek and whispered into his ear.

"Hope's act of love removing those bullets might have helped save your soul from eternal damnation today, and that's a maybe! You must ask for forgiveness for all your sins, especially the sinful act you attempted today, John. Repent, John, while you still can!" she warned sternly. He looked at her with cold eyes. She returned an even more defiant glare. John roughly yanked on the horse's reins, showing his discontent.

"Come on, Maribel!" He walked away without comment thinking selfishly to himself. *Who put you in charge, lady?*

"John, we need to talk!" Hope proposed again as he walked away in anger. She could feel his resentment pushing her away.

Jeremiah got uneasy seeing Angela's scornful face. She was so angry, tears filled her eyes. He took out a handkerchief. Playfully, he drummed up an Irish accent to try to cheer her up.

"What be the matter, me Lassie? Has that young rogue upset you, me lady?" He flirted and calmed her as he wiped the tears of rage from her angry face. "Now, now, me precious, pay no attention to the young lad. We do not want these tears to freeze up on that pretty face of yours. The frost out here will freeze them solid and leave you tattooed with ice-burned Leprechaun tears! We wouldn't want that, now, would we, me pretty?"

His funny accent and smiling, dark handsome face made Angela produce a sad grin. This being their first time alone together, he gently pecked her face, kissing away the cold tears and ending on her ready lips! She abruptly pulled back and tenderly took hold of his hand.

"Please, please, Jeremiah—stop. With much grief in my heart, I have something unwelcome to tell you. Seth and Mattie are no longer with us. They have passed on to glory and now sit beside our Lord in Heaven."

Hearing this tragic news, he became angry and belligerent. Looking suddenly wild, he screamed "WHAT SAY YOU? No, no, what you speak cannot be so. I knew we should have never left them alone. We should have brought them with us. Your friend lied to me, telling me they would be safe! Maybe it is true what the sheriff accuses you of being— some type of evil black witches! The fact you just walked right out from my dreams into my life is more evidence! What evil nightmare has this become? Have you placed me under one of your evil black spells, witch? What are you? What happened in the store with the sheriff?" He angrily challenged Angela. He looked toward Mariah to see the black smoke lingering in the dimming sky above the trees.

"Oh, my God, what have I done?" Closing his eyes, he broke down in grief.

Angela took hold of his hands again. "They are in a better place and have served their purpose here on earth, Jeremiah. I know it is hard to accept or even understand right now, but take solace in the fact that Heaven does exist." Her pleading voice sounded miles away as she tried to console him.

Jeremiah looked back up to the black cloud in the sky and snatched his hands out of her grasp.

"I need no sympathy from the likes of you! Seth and Mattie were the only two people that I ever cared about and now they are dead!" He lashed out, placing blame on himself. "I should have stayed or brought them with us. They were supposed to be at the church for the celebration anyway! Why did I not insist on getting them out of harm's way and bring them along? I just sat there and did what you told me to do. As the sheriff accused you, you newcomers might well be evil!"

"Jeremiah, this was all his work of deception and evil misdirection. Sheriff Joppa is behind all of this! For whatever reason, Hope's spell did not hold. His evil is a lot stronger than we could have ever imagined."

Jeremiah was not hearing any of it. His eyes were tight as he spoke grimly. "John was right—he should have killed him when he had the chance!"

John and Hope returned, running back after hearing Jeremiah's loud outpour of rage. He turned to confront them as they walked up. The venom of revenge tasted bittersweet in his mouth. His focused, turning on Hope, pointing a threatening finger in her face.

"And you, little miss prissy cat acting all cute and innocent! You broke your promise! You lied to me and said that no harm would come to them!" He pointed up in anger at the black clouds morbidly coiling in the distance. He turned back to Angela, adding her to his scorn. "You must had me under a spell, woman, for me to leave them alone, unprotected like that after whatever it was that happened inside the store with the sheriff! I should have never taken you to meet them in the first place! They were two of the most loving, kindest people that ever lived. All of you have lied to me and it's because of the lot of you they are dead!"

John went ballistic hearing for the first time that Sheriff Joppa has murdered Seth and Mattie.

"Oh no, are you telling me the sheriff done went and killed Seth and Mattie? Oh, hell no! I know the hatred that I see in your eyes, Jeremiah. That bastard killed my momma and daddy, too! You remember what we talked about, partner! We need to go back and finish our business with that red neck bastard. I swear he is a dead man now, and nobody better try to stop me!"

"I'm with you, my brother! Let's rid the earth of this evil monster!" Jeremiah readily agreed. They trotted past the women at a fast pace back toward Mariah to reap their vengeance. Hope shouted out after them.

"No! Hear me now, the both of you! It is imperative that we stay together and get the child to the sanctuary of the church before darkness falls or all will be lost. You will not prevail against the Moloch Leader; he is not human but a demon in disguise!"

CHAPTER 17

A Rude Awakening

Totally ignoring Hope's plea, the two angry men began running back toward town. Angela suddenly appeared on the trail in front of them. Her golden swords, drawn, were pointing directly at them. The men stopped as she grimly gave warning. "Hear me! You both shall perish under the hand of Ezekiel Joppa. He will kill you if you go back there!"

The two young fools paid no heed to the women's warnings and took a step forward. Angela stood her ground in front of Jeremiah.

"Stop, Jeremiah, I beg of you, I know well the pain you feel. I met the same pain when death claimed both my parents separately. I was present and felt the pain again when John lost his parents. They were my closest friends, murdered in a most horrible death due to this same vile man. He killed Easter's mother and has taken other innocent lives for generations. He is looking to kill the child and all of us given the chance. Jeremiah, I ask that you do not do this. Do not fall prey like John to an obsession of revenge against the sheriff. Joppa is trying cloud to your purpose the same way he has twisted John. I need you with me by my side when we face the battle that comes. However, first you must fight the battle within yourself. Make good your worthiness with forgiveness and prove your resolve through faith and doing what is right!"

Compassion flowed from her eyes.

"Lastly, my love, the final most important confession I make to you is that if I am your guardian angel, as you know in your heart that I am, then you must accept the fact that I myself have died. I do know all too well the pain of death. You must believe that in this tragedy there is rejoicing in what has occurred. Your returning to town will compromise everything! This I cannot allow and should you not heed my warning, you will certainly die. Do not force my hand to do battle with you." Her tearfully bitter cold-steel stare silently dared them to take another step forward. She took a battle stance.

Hope suddenly appeared next to her, with the child in her arms. She set the baby down and drew her golden sword, ready to do battle. John and Jeremiah look at one another then to the women standing defiantly in front of them. Angela's eyes met Jeremiah's. He hated to admit her gaze was spellbinding. Angela slowly sheathed her swords.

"Trust me, Jeremiah, please take my hand."

"Hold your hand just so you can cast me under another spell? What's wrong, did your magic wear off like your friend's over there?"

"You know in your heart, my darling, I am no voodoo witch as accused and I am truly your guardian angel. What you do at this crossroads is your choice and of your own free will. I ask that you put your hatred aside and stand by me, my love. Be righteous. Come with us, Jeremiah."

Taking a look up at the huge, black cloud over the town, he sheathed his sword, reaching out to take Angela's hand. A blue aura from above covered his body in a black robe, thus joining Jeremiah to them as a righteous warrior.

"Oh, Jeremiah, I love you so much. Thank you, thank you, my Lord, amen, amen!" Angela hugged and kissed him, surprising everyone, including herself.

"Amen!" the three repeated. However, infuriated, John said nothing. He retrieved Maribel and looked at Jeremiah with disgust and disappointment. "You mean to tell me you're going to let him get away with killing Seth and Mattie that easily? Loves don't have anything to do with this! We need to go kill that man!"

Jeremiah, now enlightened, stopped him with a stern "WAIT." Without looking back out from under the hood, he spoke.

"It has everything to do with it, don't you understand? Let it go and get on board, John! There is more to all this than just the sheriff. Let it go!" He helped Angela and the child mount.

John turned and stared angrily in the direction of Mariah, then to Jeremiah leading the others in the opposite direction. Hope, still standing next to him, said, "John . . . look at me!" Still resisting, John bit his bottom lip and avoided her. She cupped his face in her hands, forcing him to look into her eyes.

"John! You are not the man you were before I left. I have seen and heard you say things that I would never have imagined. What has been going on? You are becoming my greatest challenge. Getting the child to the church is all that matters for us right at this moment! It is not about your love for me and it is certainly not about getting revenge on the sheriff! Stay with us. Do not leave me now, I beg of you. Seek your atonement, John! Things will be all right if you just do the right thing!"

His tight grip on his weapon loosened. Slowly, he put away his sword. She sheathed her weapon, too, and took John into her arms. As they hugged, her mind's eye revealed a horrid secret John has kept hidden from all of them. Shocked by what she has discovered, Hope broke away from their embrace. She was deeply disturbed and troubled. Were Angela to learn of this secret, she would surely kill him on the spot. The child, Easter, began screaming. Angela grabbed Hope's arm.

"Come quickly, we must move, now!"

No one spoke another word; they walked in silence until they reached the clearing. They arrived at the Church of God just before the sun drifted underneath the horizon. Most of the townsfolk had arrived and were getting ready inside for the christening.

The bell was properly placed back and secured in the steeple, and Reverend Bishop stood smiling with his arms folded in front of the completed church. He was pleased.

A cold, strong wind whipped through the clearing just as Jeremiah and the others stepped out of the woods.

"Jeremiah and the newcomers are returning!" the sentry shouted.

The Reverend turned, happy to see them crossing the clearing. Surprisingly, the majority of townsfolk gathered warmly to greet them. The reverend happily walked over, shouting to them gleefully. He noticed that Jeremiah was now dressed like the others, wearing a black robe.

"Well, well, welcome back, new friends! We thought you had left us. I am happy to see you all return in time for our celebration this evening. Jeremiah, where are Seth and Mattie? They should have been here hours ago!"

Jeremiah gave him a look of remorse, still unable to speak of the tragedy. Angela stepped up, speaking quietly to the Reverend.

"Uhh, Reverend Bishop ... can we all go somewhere to speak privately? Jeremiah is in mourning. The sheriff has murdered his uncle and aunt. It happened about an hour ago; their store was deliberately set on fire. He approaches now to capture this child, to kill us and anyone else that stands in his way. Jeremiah needs your condolence and would do well with your prayers right now. Find comfort that Seth and Mattie now sit in Heaven's court with our Lord."

The Reverend reared back in shock and immediately announced to the townsfolk.

"Please give me one minute with Jeremiah and our visitors, please!" They exited together into the back of the church.

"Seth and Mattie are dead? Killed by Sheriff Joppa, you say? My Lord, no, it can't be!" His eyes misted hearing of the loss of his good friends at the hands of the ruthless sheriff. "My Lord, why they were the ones that fixed and donated the shoes I passed out earlier. They were good Christians doing whatever they could to help others. They were good colored folk to those in need. I grew a bit fretful when they did not show up here to participate. Come, we will go into the church office for a moment."

Behind closed doors, Angela took over and explained further.

"The man whom you know as your County Sheriff, Ezekiel Joppa, is much more than what he seems. He follows and worships the darkest of evil. He is a Moloch!"

"A Moloch, you say! My, my, the evil you speak of is not hard to believe. Yes, yes, of course! We know well of the wretched heathens that stalk these woods."

Angela walked over to Jeremiah, taking hold of the child bundled up in his arms.

"It was getting a bit chilly out, so I covered her up," Jeremiah spoke in a tender, fatherly tone.

Hope took the reverend's hand into hers. Unwrapping the robe from around the child, Angela told him, "She is a newborn."

Surprised, the reverend asked, "You mean to say this child was born recently?"

"Last night," Angela calmly replied.

Still under the impression that the child was Angela's daughter, the reverend looked at Angela with amazement.

"This is a miracle, I must say! She is the biggest newborn baby I have ever seen! She must weigh near two stone."

He turned and with much sympathy in his voice complimented Angela. "You are to be commended, child! But, I must say, it does puzzle me that you don't look like a woman who has just given birth last night to such a big, healthy child!"

"Reverend, she is not my child. Her mother passed while giving her life. She is orphaned!" Angela told him truthfully.

Hope interceded. "Yes, however, she is a very special child. With faith as strong as yours, Reverend, it will be easy for you to see."

He gazed in wonderment at his awakening as the epiphany revealed itself before his eyes.

"Oh, my Lord, Jesus, I see the true spirit of the child. I must tell everyone of this." The reverend rejoiced.

Hope calmed the reverend and explained their precarious situation to him.

"Please, Reverend! For now, the child only reveals her true self to you. The others cannot see her as you do. They will become aware in time and on time; now is not the right time. We here in Mariah must protect this child and stand in battle against the evil that comes. A spiritual battle is about to begin here. Even now, as we speak, Sheriff Joppa approaches, with many following!"

"For generations, my family has spoken of Good and Evil spiritual battles that take place here on earth. How are we to stand and fight against something unholy such this? We have no weapons to battle with here. What about my parishioners, what will happen to them?" He asked, gravely concerned about their safety.

"You said you believe in miracles, didn't you Reverend Bishop?" Angela asked, smiling.

"Yes, of course, my child!"

"Then I promise you that tonight you will witness miracles as none have ever seen. Just stay strong in what you choose to believe, Reverend."

"I will not waver when the miracle you speak of arrives! The congregation waits anxiously to hear what is going on. Will it be all right if we just act normal for now?" the reverend asked.

"Yes, but I don't know how much time we have," Hope replied.

"Then we would like to proceed with the christening and celebrations as planned. I would like you to meet the children that are in my charge, for I fear for their safety the most."

"I would like that very much, Reverend Bishop."

CHAPTER 18

Out of the Mouths of Babes

"For the celebration, we have scheduled quite a treat. Our orphans are a major part of the youth choir. I have named them, "The Lord's Psalms" and they have prepared to sing to us tonight for the first time. I am looking forward to it. This should make for quite a show of talent. Come, let me show you how truly blessed they are," he boasted proudly. He led them over to the children gathered nearby and called out the names of two young ones.

"Kristen, Corey, come over here please." The two children ran over to the group. Reverend Bishop turned to Hope.

"Ask them to recite any Psalm. Corey, you will be first."

The biracial boy with the prettiest blue crossed eyes and a bushy head full of brown, curly hair let out a little sigh. He was no more than eleven or twelve years old. The girl, Kristen, obviously his brown-eyed older sister with a head full of bronze curly locks, stepped up next to him and gave him a playful nudge. He turned and stuck out his tongue at his sister, and her friend, Jessica, standing next to her, sheepishly stepped to the front.

"Ready?" Hope asked. Corey nodded.

"Okay, Corey, I would like for you to recite Psalm 25 for me."

Corey squinted his eyes tightly as he looked over at his sister and Jessica. They giggled at him, whispering to each other, teasing him. He turned and opened his eyes wide, causing them to cross even more. "Did you say all of it, ma'am?"

"Just the first eleven verses," Hope responded, feeling sorry for the cute, caramel colored, curly haired, cross-eyed boy, who was in terrible need of a pair of glasses.

Corey let out a sigh of relief and closed his eyes again. There was a long pause as if he was searching for the passages. He held his hands in prayer and began:

"Psalm 25. Unto thee, O' Lord, I pray ... I trust in thee be ashamed . . . Oh, goodness!" He paused immediately, realizing his mistake. Kristen and Jessica burst out laughing at the boy's flub. Corey's face saddened, he was obviously embarrassed by his misquote.

"No, no, that's not right ... ma'am ... umm, Reverend, can I please start over again?" He asked. Getting a little flustered, he started rubbing his left eye, a nervous habit.

"It is all right, Corey, take your time and start again. Children, God don't like ugly and you all are acting mighty ugly right now!" Reverend Bishop scolded, eyeballing them with a stern look.

"Yes, son, go right ahead whenever you're ready, Corey."

Corey cupped his hands, closed his eyes and began again reciting the psalm's eleven verses.

He finished without error, everyone clapping and giving praise to the young man for a job well done. Angela and Hope looked at John, disappointed that he was not paying any attention to the boy's recital, which was meant for him. The townswomen women flirted with and distracted him. The reverend praised Corey's recital.

"That was flawless, Corey, all perfect verses, excellent job!" Hope walked over to the young boy, clapping enthusiastically.

"You should have a reward for doing such a good job." She brushed the top of Corey's curly hair. "Let us see what gift the Lord has placed in my pocket for you. Do you like candy?" she asked.

"Yes!" Corey smiled.

She searched her robe, finding a pocket. She hesitated, looking puzzled.

"Oh, I think I have something sweet, but not to taste!"

What could she be talking about? Corey wondered. She slowly pulled out a pair of small, wire-rimmed bifocals. Wide eyed and grinning at the sight of the eyeglasses, he was speechless. He put them on and for the first time in his young life, things were no longer fuzzy and blurred. He clearly saw everyone's faces. He looked around while a broad, ecstatic smile spread across his face. His vision was sharp and clear and his big, beautiful blue eyes were now set straight and proper! His eyes were no longer impaired. A miracle had come true for the boy.

"I told you.... Are those sweet, or what? Huh?" Hope said.

"Goodness!" he shouted in glee. "Yeess ... these are SWEET! Thank you, pretty lady!"

"You are very welcome, young man." Hope chuckled. "It is a small reward for such a great presentation!"

Beaming with joy, he ran over to Kristen and Jessica. Seeing their faces clearly for the first time, Corey teased his pretty sister.

"Oh! I knew you were ugly, but I did not know you were *that* ugly!

"Aww, forget you, talking about ugly! Wait until you see yourself in a mirror!" She lovingly bumped up against him. He tripped, causing his glasses to fling off his face and strike hard against a big rock.

"Kristen!" he shouted in desperate anguish.

"Oh, Corey, I am so sorry!" Kristen knew how precious the glasses were to her little brother.

He picked up the glasses. Holding them high up in the air for all to see, he smiled and said, "Na na na na na ... they're not broken!"

Hope winked at him. He returned a big smile, proudly putting his glasses back on.

"Nanny- nanny-na-na!" he teased his sister again, this time sticking his tongue out.

"Glad I didn't break 'em. Now go find a mirror so you can see how ugly you really are," Kristen teased back, relieved.

Reverend Bishop intervened. "Hey, now, that's enough of that. Kristen, it's your turn."

"READY!" The brash young girl responded.

Pausing for a minute to pray, she closed her eyes and began spinning in a circle pointing randomly at everyone gathered around. She stopped at John and in a loud and commanding voice, picked up Psalms 25 at verse 11:

"But Lord, my sins! How many they are. Oh, pardon them for the honor of Your name. Where is the man who fears the Lord?"

She stared at John, then Jeremiah, before continuing to recite to the crowd. The young girl turned away, and finished acting out the rest of the psalm in front of her audience, with dramatic style. When she got to the last line of the psalm, Kristin finished her act by dropping down to one knee, as if in prayer, right in front of John.

"Assign me godliness and integrity, for I expect you to protect me and to redeem Israel oh God, from all their troubles!"

As everyone clapped with enthusiastic appreciation, Kristen stood, smiling provocatively at John.

Hope congratulated her, totally impressed. Kristen took a long bow.

"Oh, I see we have a little performer in the making, here! That was an excellent presentation!" Hope turned to John, who was inattentive, his mind drifting somewhere else.

"What do you think about what you just heard, John?" she asked him.

"No way could I have recited psalms like that when I was their age. Their talent is amazing."

"I was talking about the psalm itself she recited, John."

"Oh yeah, yeah, that was deep, very deep," he patronized her.

Hope frowned at his remark. She turned back to the little girl and searched her robe pocket again for a prize.

Kristen tugged at Hope's robe and motioned her to come closer so she could whisper something in her ear.

"I don't need eye glasses, ma'am," she innocently informed her.

"I know," Hope replied, pulling out something wrapped in brown paper.

"It's something just for you, but don't be selfish with it." She unwrapped the gift and unveiled four large sticks of candy cane. Kristen could not remember the last time she had had store-bought candy. She looked over to the Reverend for approval. He nodded with a smile.

"Be mindful of what she said about sharing!"

Kristen readily accepted the candy from Hope.

"Oh, thank you, ma'am!"

"That should last you a while."

Frowning, Kristen pointed over at her brother and the other children. They waited anxiously, drooling in anticipation of sharing her sweet reward.

"I'm not going to have much left after I share it with everyone," she pouted.

"One or two pieces should be enough for everyone. You will see when you share it." Hope had a twinkle in her eye.

"Thank you, ma'am, I'll remember to share! What is your name?" the young girl asked, revealing an innocently wise and quite charming personality.

"My name is Hope, Hope Matthews."

"Like the book of Matthew! Thank you for the candy, Hope Matthews! I am Kristen, Kristen Henry, and that curly head boy you gave the glasses to over there is my brother, Corey. I can tell you we are most thankful for the gifts, ma'am." The child looked oddly at Hope. "You chose that psalm to send a message to the one named John, didn't you? He is hiding something terribly bad, you know!" She showed Hope a puzzled frown, curtsied and then ran over toward the other gathered children. Hope knew well the wisdom the child spoke. The girl shouted teasingly to her gathered friends.

"Wheeee! Who wants candy?" She quickly darted off, holding the candy canes high in the air. The children chased after her yelling and screaming in joy. She led them over to a big tree stump. Candy crazed, they surrounded her, jumping around up and down with outstretched arms and open hands, calling out her name for attention.

"Give me your scarf, Jessica." She wrapped two whole sticks of candy cane in the scarf and slammed it down hard upon the stump. She dramatically opened up the scarf revealing nice-sized pieces of sweet candy cane, more than enough for everyone.

Meanwhile, the adults in the crowd began to mumble uncomfortably again, after seeing Hope's little tricks, igniting new suspicions about the odd set of strangers.

The reverend spoke proudly of his two presenters. "The children are truly gifted aren't they?"

"I must say, Kristen and Corey sure are special, that's for sure! They are blessed with amazing vision and wisdom for children their age."

"Out of the mouths of babes, just as the good book says!" "Now I'll tell you what was amazing, young lady, was the way you pulled those gifts out from your pockets." Reverend Bishop probed.

She had not even known the robe had pockets, much less that they'd produce such specific gifts. Hope tried to explain. "I just happen to come across things as we make our journey. There is something else, Reverend Bishop," Hope added. "We have a gift for the church. I was hoping that we could present it to you and the congregation at the celebration tonight."

"That would be most glorious!" the Reverend replied. "Consider our church your sanctuary—you will be safe here!" He turned the conversation to John.

"Now, John, earlier, before you all left, you were telling me about your family here and what place you all came from? What's the name of your church?" the Reverend asked.

John was caught totally off guard by the question; he fumbled to respond just as a little boy ran up to Reverend Bishop, excited and out of breath. He tugged impatiently on the reverend's long robe.

"Excuse me, Reverend Bishop, Deacon Phillips says for you to come now so you can test the bell!"

"Fine, fine, yes, yes." He took hold of the little boy's hand. "Come, Brother Jacob, we must make sure there are no cracks." Walking away, he turned to John with a wry smile.

"Please, excuse me. We'll have our talk later, John."

"Yes, of course, Reverend!" John readily agreed, relieved at the reprieve. He meant to be prepared if asked again.

CHAPTER 19

Angela's Prayer

Everyone gathered excitedly in the large front hall under the steeple tower and spilling out of the front of the building. They happily awaited the reverend to begin the christening of the church.

"In the name of God, his son, Jesus Christ, and the Holy Spirit, we anoint this township of Mariah as God's Country. From this day forth, let no evil tread upon these holy church grounds. We toll this bell in honor of all the unknown Negro soldiers whom during the civil war fell in the terrible battle fought here. Buried without a prayer, you called me here to build your church in their honor, and we now pray that their souls rest peacefully in the name of God."

The people gathered sounded cheers of amens and halleluiahs. He bowed his head then gestured the sign of the crucifix. He grabbed hold of the thick, dangling bell rope and the hall grew silent. He tugged on it forcibly, and the congregation laughed as the rope lifted his short, pudgy frame up off the floor. When no ring sounded, everyone looked concerned and worried.

"Put a little more faith into it, Reverend." A friendly taunt came from a female in the cheerful crowd.

"Put some more muscle into it, Reverend!" an unseen male shouted jokingly from the belfry.

"Give him strength, Lord!" Deacon Phillips praised, bringing more smiles and chuckles of laughter from the congregation.

The Reverend spit into his hands rubbed them together and gave the bell a mighty tug. This time, the bell responded with a loud, righteous ring as he rode the rope like a yo-yo.

A joyous atmosphere sprung to life at the sound, a sound that would never fail to bring joy to the hearts of men. Shouts of praise rose from the congregation. Another loud ring followed. People sang and hugged. Some cried tears of joy, kicking off the celebration.

"Thank you, Lord! Thank you, Jesus!" The reverend praised as he jumped down off the rope.

"Now, it's your turn." The reverend offered Jeremiah a turn at ringing the bell.

Jeremiah stepped up to the rope. He looked over to Angela. She smiled at him, and lifted the baby for him to see. Easter waved her little hand at him, putting a large grin on Jeremiah's face. He gave the rope one mighty yank,making the bell produce a double ring. The congregation roared with delight, shouting out in amazement.

Bewildered, the reverend looked on in awe.

"That was for Seth and Mattie," he somberly told the holy man.

"Good God a mighty, Jeremiah!" Reverend Bishop turned to the congregation. "The man has the strength of Samson in them arms!"

Though many tried after him, no man was able to strike the bell the way Jeremiah had.

* * *

In the woods nearby, Anthony has led Sheriff Joppa and the two deputies to the church. The first clang of the church bell exploded inside of Joppa's head. Bent over in his saddle, covering his ears in pain, he howled and grimaced as the ringing echoed through his evil skull. He cursed the sound and retreated angrily, shouting to the boy to deliver an ultimatum.

"You go and tell those black bastards what I told you, that I'm hunting them voodoo witches for the murders of Seth and Mattie Stone. I'll be back, and if they aren't standing outside waiting when I return, I will burn their church down and kill every Negro protecting them!"

The sheriff and his deputies disappeared into the woods, trying desperately to out ride the sound of the blasphemous bell. The ringing bell had no effect on Anthony, who now served the Moloch. Laughing, he turned and ran across the clearing toward the church as commanded.

Meanwhile, inside the church, Angela warned Hope.

"John has yet to confess! Should he not do this before this battle begins he will be the first to feel my blades. You know as well as I he must answer for all the wrong he has done, Hope."

"John will not be with us for this battle tonight. His time here is ended." Hope gave Angela some unexpected news.

"I have known of his challenges from the beginning; he must atone," Angela responded.

Hope replied somberly, "His was the greatest challenge, Angela. He has used up his time here with us. He is to have a final opportunity to make right everything through my sister, Faith, when he returns to their future time!"

"Return to Mariah ... but of what good is he to be once he is back there? He will very well put Faith and your mother in harm's way upon his return. Maybe he will even cause the battle to be lost in the future, when both must be won!" Angela protested in vain.

"He deserves another chance! He needs Faith! He returns before this hour is over!" Hope ordered.

Suddenly, they were alarmed, feeling Ezekiel's approach with his nefarious minions. As they prepared, Angela wondered about Hope's mention of John's test being truly the greatest when compared to her own love quagmire with That Guy. She looked at Jeremiah, who turned to her.

"Merry Christmas, Angela! I could not ask for a better gift than you being here with me this day.... I truly do love you, angel of my dreams!"

She smiled back at him in total bliss, saying nothing. She never felt or loved a man this way before. She had died before attaching too emotionally to any one man, except her father. That Guy in her dreams was the only man she had ever truly felt a woman's love for. At this moment, standing next to the big handsome brother and holding the baby in her arms made her heart flutter. *Just when I thought it was impossible to fall any more in love with him, That Guy goes and says something like that!* He took her by the hand.

"Will you look at all this joy and love? I just wish Seth and Mattie were here with us." They observed the joyous celebration around them. His eyes and expression grew solemn; he let go of her hand and stared off into the distance. Angela saw his aunt and uncle's spiritual images smiling happily, nodding acknowledgment to her. As they faded away into the crowd, Angela squeezed Jeremiah hand in hers.

"They are here, Jeremiah. They are right here with us." She placed a tender hand over his heart. He looked down at the child, Easter, in her arms, smiling up at him.

"May I hold her?" Jeremiah asked for the first time.

"Of course you can!" Angela happily gave him the child, and he kissed her fondly on the forehead.

"I feel so close to this child and you, it is as if you were my family ... like you both were my own."

"So do I, Jeremiah."

"I have something I would like to ask of you, Angela." Sadly she already knew what he was about to ask. This was more than she could bear right now. She closed her eyes, holding back the tears, knowing if not in battle, all this will soon end anyway, taking her far away from him, the child and this place. Overwhelmed with anxiety, she made a request.

"Please excuse me, Jeremiah before you ask your question, all this excitement has made me a little light headed. I need to go outside for a moment and get some air. Can you watch over Easter until I return?"

"I will go with you. My duty calls for me to watch and protect you and the child at all times."

"No, no, Jeremiah. I need a private moment, please," Angela persisted. She moved her body in a way suggesting that she had to use the outhouse. "You understand!"

"Oh? Oh, yes, yes, of course, my angel!" Jeremiah turned twenty shades of red. "Just hurry back, I have something very important to share with you!"

She nodded and quickly exited the celebration. Angela stood alone outside in the graveyard. Cold northern winds blew around her. Big, warm tears rolled down her cheeks as she sadly covered her head with her hood. She prayed.

"I do not question what has to be done here, but I am so confused. This man came to me in my dreams when I was a mortal woman, and I foolishly fell in love with him then. His looks of desire burn inside of me wickedly! I grow weaker by the minute, wanting to surrender and give him all of me. Why is the one man I have no power not to love returned to me here? Already I feel pain, knowing I must leave him when all this is over." She broke down.

Someone else was crying next to her. Startled, she opened her eyes. Hope stood, offered comfort.

"Amen to that! As you said yourself, Angela, we all are to be tested! I never could have imagined that the challenge would come between the ones we care and love the most."

The two stood together in silence as the bell tolled. Hope took hold of Angela's hand.

"It has started!" Hope whispered, placing her hood on her head.

"Bring it, Evil One! Your executioner awaits you!" Angela shouted, challenging the night.

The echo of her threat carried loudly over the cold, silent valley. A broad smile came to Joppa's face as Angela's challenge reached his ears. Behind him followed his army of dead souls.

The two rejoined the festive celebration inside, looking like grim reapers. Eating and talking, the congregation sat together on the rows of pews and tables. Many stopped and cast a fretful eye at the robed women.

"Witches," someone said loudly from behind her half-covered face. A few women pulled their napkins or handkerchiefs to their faces, turning their heads and eyes away in fear. Hearing the slanderous remark, others began to focus negatively on the black hooded robes moving through the crowd.

Reaching their table, they briefly spoke to the three men, then all swept into the reverend's office to speak privately. The congregation went back to eating, celebrating and, of course, spreading rumors about.

"Is everything all right, my children? Is there something wrong?" Hope took the reverend by the hand.

"There is a lot you must understand in a short amount of time! Do not fear what I am about to reveal. Before this hour is over, miracles will appear. Those who are strong in their faith will see and hear the truth tonight."

Angela explained further.

"This is Judgment Day for all of us gathered here today, Reverend. We must prepare to take part in the battle that draws nigh. Those here are here for this very reason. This is the true purpose of their calling to Mariah, to play their role in this battle!

"We don't have much time. The sheriff quickly approaches. He brings legions of lost souls with him. We must prepare to take part in the fight against evil."

The humble reverend sat in awe of all he has heard. He acknowledged her revelation.

"Reverend, we need to go and inform the congregation that they should prepare for what is about to occur. We shall immediately address them after that. Does anyone have anything else to say?" She and Hope looked to John. Angela's eyes turned cold and emotionless as John said nothing. The men paused briefly, then walked toward the door. Hope's eyes teared up. A mean scowl crossed Angela's face, filled with anger.

PART 3

Trials, Tribulations And Judgment Day

CHAPTER 20

Party Poopers

Hope caught John by the arm and pulled him back into the office to be alone.

"John, there is something, something very important that I must tell you...." He placed a finger lightly on Hope's lips, stopping her from delivering her message.

"Sure, but I have something to confess to *you* first!"

Anxiously, she waited hoping what he had to say was the right thing.

"Hope, I've missed you so. I did not realize how much I loved you until that day you died. Now we have a second chance being back here, together again...." This was not the confession she needed to hear. She slapped him.

"I am not the one! Oh, my God, John, why are you trying to ignore what is really going on here?" His admission of love makes her stomach turn. "You will return to Mariah to join Faith and my mother in the battle about to take place there. You . . .you must confess everything to Faith and ask forgiveness immediately once you return!" She demanded, distraught. "Angela, Jeremiah and I will stay to do battle here. Please, John! Do the right thing and confess all to Faith, John ... and I mean everything!"

John, full of contempt and resentment, felt betrayed by Hope's rejection. In addition, how could he confess everything to Faith without losing her also?

"Now, go and get the cross, John. It stays here with us. We are to present it as a gift it to Reverend Bishop and the church." Her request ripped into John like a bolt of lightning.

"How was I to know I would ever be going back, Hope?" he shouted at her, confused and dumbfounded.

"Go get it, now, John! There is not much time before our battle begins and I have to warn and prepare the others here of what is about to happen." Tears streamed down her face as she ran out of the office into the church. She left John immersed in anger. *I can't believe this! How was I to guess that I would be returning home to Faith? And, if I do leave the cross here, how am I supposed to fight in battle when I get back without my weapon?* Grudgingly, though, he followed her orders, holding the holy crucifix in his hands. A soft wind brushed his cheek, whispering, "Without Hope, there is nothing!" He looked around, surprised by the voice. His gaze drifted up to the foothills. A long trail of torches approached.

John rushed back inside the church to inform every one of the coming danger. Hope, seeing John's urgency, quickly turned back to the reverend.

"Miracles are about to be witnessed. John will be leaving us shortly, and he has brought you a parting gift."

John stepped up and handed the large metal crucifix over to the reverend.

"I present this altar cross as our gift to you and the Church of God. This cross is truly a gift from God. "John glanced at Hope, looking for a sign of approval of his presentation and compliance with her orders. She paid him no notice.

"Thank you so much, my son ... a miracle come true! The Lord told me he would send us a blessing tonight. I am elated and overjoyed by your precious donation to our church. A church without an altar cross is like having faith without hope." Reverend Bishop continued with the dedication.

John nudged his head slightly toward the office and silently mouthed to Hope, "I need to talk to you!"

Frowning, Hope held up a finger signaling him to wait. Giving her a cross look of impatience he stepped over and whispered into her ear.

"I have something very important I got to tell you!"

"Not now, John, please! I know of Joppa's arrival."

"No ... right now, Hope!" John demanded whispering back into her ear. He grabbed her by the arm. Both glared in defiance at one another. The Reverend Bishop, noticing the two having words, interrupted, stepping between them. He took hold of John's hand. Hope used the opportunity to step away. The reverend cradled the heavy metal cross humbly, like a baby, and made an announcement to the congregation.

"Thank you so much again, my son. Now, let us take a quick break, clean up and place the pews back in order. It is time to have a service!"

The parishioners began putting the church back in order. Meanwhile, behind closed doors, Hope and the others decided how to address the congregation. They came out and Reverend Bishop began his sermon.

"I know this sounds hard to believe, but believe you must. Tonight we all will stand witness to miracles and the purpose of our true calling to Mariah! Do you truly believe in God? Raise your hand and praise him if you do!"

All gathered raised their hands and said, "AMEN" in unison.

"If this is true, you must believe in miracles."

A few uncomfortable amens bounced around the church. Having everyone's attention, the reverend was about to speak on the deaths of Seth and Mattie.

Suddenly, bursting through the heavy wooden doors a tremendous cold blast of wind made its howling entrance. Everybody turned to the back of the church. The young boy, Anthony, stood at the front doors, hollering as if he were crazy. Sneering, he shouted at the three newcomers standing at the altar of the church.

"Murderers! The newcomers are evil witches, y'all! They kilt Seth and Mattie. I saw them work their black magic myself! They didn't know I was watching them through the back door of the general store. Uh huh ...yup, that's right, I was there ... I saw you! I saw everything!" The Reverend shouts out to the boy. "Anthony what are you saying? Come inside here, my son." He pushed his way through the crowd of people, who saw that he was bloody and had been beaten very badly.

The reverend ran from the pulpit to the boy. "Anthony, what in God's name has happened to you, son? What are you talking about?"

Pointing them out, the boy glared evilly at Hope, John and Angela. "They burned Seth and Mattie alive in the general store ... that's right, the store's gone, too ... burnt right down to the ground with them in it still alive!" he vehemently lied.

Gasps of shock and woe erupted, filling the church. Possessed by the sheriff's power, Anthony gave a stellar performance. The sheriff would be pleased.

The church grew dark and hostile. The once-festive group quickly turned into an angry, grief-stricken lynch mob. Those standing near the newcomers began to back away. Blood drooled from his mouth as the boy continued with his lying accusations.

"They are black witches. Yeah, they did it and that ain't all! I even saw that one perform some evil blue magic and beat down the sheriff." He pointed directly to Angela. He then pointed a shaking finger over at Hope. "And that one helped beat down the sheriff's deputies; the witches' hands glowed when they whispered into Seth and Mattie's ears and put a spell on them!" Finally, he pointed to John. "He tried to kill the sheriff with a shotgun while he lay knocked out on the floor! The sheriff told me they kidnapped that baby, cut her right out her momma's womb. He said that Jeremiah was walking around under a witch's spell—placed on him by that one over there with the funny colored hair. That is why the sheriff is leading a large posse of men here right now, to come and arrest them all!"

He turned to all the others.

"He told me to warn y'all about these strangers. They all are evil black witches going around passing themselves off as some kind of holy people. When I found out the strangers killed Seth and Mattie, I felt obligated to bring 'em. I just had to, Reverend Bishop! When we got here he let me go and told me to run up ahead and warn that no harm will come to anybody if those three over there gives themselves up and turns over the child they stole unharmed. Please forgive me, Reverend! His deputies whipped me and threatened to lynch me if I did not tell him where they were heading and show them where the church is."

Anthony broke down in tears, peeping at John's Nikes before burying his bloody face into the Reverend's robe. People gathered around the boy protectively. Someone covered his body with a blanket.

"Don't you fret any, Anthony, you couldn't help yourself. You are safe here with us now. We need to tend to your wounds, son."

The Reverend comforted the boy, not believing a word he'd spoken. The boy paused to look around at everyone before delivering the final threat. The wind filled with the sound of wolves as he looked outside through the open back doors.

"He swore if they ain't standing outside the church by the time he arrives, he is gonna burn this church down and kill every Niggro up in here! He said no one is safe from those black voodoo followers and their evil spells. The sheriff is riding up right behind me ... coming down the trail right now. You had better get them voodoo priestesses out of here, Reverend."

"Did da boy say voodoo priestesses?" a woman with a Jamaican accent shouted. The congregation rumbled uncomfortably in fear of the boy's allegations.

"Witches they be, I say, I knew there was something strange' bout them girls, especially her!" She pointed directly at Angela. Hearing the woman's comments from the back of the church, Leotis shouted out, "I told you it was something peculiar and odd about them ... them perdestrians!"

Reverend Bishop attempted to quell the situation and head off the makings of an all-out witch-hunt before it got any more out of control. He spoke sternly in defense of the newcomers.

"Now, just hold on, everybody! Wait a minute, here! We cannot be so quick to pass judgment on what this boy accuses without hearing from those that he accuses. I personally vouch for our newcomers. They are no evil murderers or voodoo witches. They have already told me of the unfortunate fate of Seth and Mattie. This is the terrible news that what I was about to speak on! The sheriff conspires against the newcomers to prevent them from exposing him as the evil killer of Seth and Mattie. This is why they have returned here for sanctuary, fleeing from him and his gun-slinging deputies! We all know how deceiving Sheriff Joppa can be. He would go to any lengths to rid not only this town, but this entire valley, of us. He hates us all for being here and he is more evil than what he poses to be.

"I denounce the claim that Jeremiah is under some type of spell, I have just heard his confessions and he is a recommitted Christian man! I ask you, is that something someone under an evil spell would do? Come into the house of the Lord, confess all his sins and repent? I think not! Please, I ask you to consider these things!" He paused. "These accusations by the sheriff are all lies to turn us against each other."

Someone yelled at the Reverend from the crowd, "That one with them funny colored braids looks like one of those African witch doctors!" The reverend found it hard to pinpoint the people doing all the derogatory shouting. Everyone's attention turned back to Angela, Hope, John and Jeremiah. Another voice filled with fear shouted up to the pulpit. "Get them witches out of here, Reverend!"

A few frightened families quietly exited the church. Everyone stared and waited in silence with great anticipation to see what would happen next.

"Y'all best be worried about that sheriff riding up here. What part of him killing everybody up in here if they ain't standing outside don't you all understand?" Anthony attempted to distract the crowd.

Jeremiah grabbed John and took him to the pulpit.

"Please, everyone, please hear me and what I have to say! Please listen to me."

The crowd quieted down out of respect.

"These people did nothing to harm Seth and Mattie. Do you think any spell could keep me from taking out my revenge upon them were they the killers! They have been in my presence since their arrival here. This is all the sheriff's doing!"

He lifted up the cross and John's arm high into the air.

"I ask you all, would a worshipper of black magic or evil practitioner of voodoo—"

A loud thunderclap boomed and inside the church a brilliant pale blue light surrounded the cross and John's body. A blinding bolt of lightning struck and John vanished. A shocking moment of frozen silence overcame the terrified crowd. Dazed, Jeremiah stood at the pulpit alone, both arms still raised, holding only the cross. Just as surprised as everyone else, the reverend found it hard to control his own anxiety. Thinking on his feet, he proclaimed, "Hallelujah, hallelujah, this was a miracle I spoke of! Please fear not and stand fast for this was our sign! Stay calm my children, be not afraid of what we witness here … trust in your faith!"

Smoke rose from the floor. Mystified, Jeremiah looked over to Reverend Bishop and he and the reverend looked down to the spot where John was just standing seconds before. The pair of unlaced white high top Nikes sat smoking. As pandemonium erupted in the aisles and pews, Reverend Bishop pled with the congregation to maintain their composure.

"Please, please! Listen everyone, do not be afraid! This was a sign from our Lord … please do not turn away!"

Hope had had enough and time was running out. She stepped up to the podium with Angela beside her and addressed the congregation.

"People! Hear what I have to say, please, I can explain what is happening! Since the beginning of everything, this valley, this town of Mariah, was a chosen as the place where good and evil battle.

"I stand before you called here to defend and do battle against the evil Moloch that approaches. You all must prepare and understand that we all were called to Mariah to partake in this day of reckoning. Tonight we will stand together and face our challenge! Your faith has to be strong and unyielding. Trust in your faith! Those of you that are true will see this truth. Look upon the child and upon Angela and me." A blue aura spun around the visitors from the future.

Anthony screamed, covering his eyes.

"Do not look! The black witch works her evil magic through the blue light! I saw her do it in the general store." He turned and ran into the crowd. A few paying heed to the boy left the church in fear.

The true believers were already bowing down in prayer. Others of his frightened congregation cowered and prayed.

The Reverend shouted out a warning, "You cannot fall victim to the rumors and false accusations made here against us. The boy Anthony is under the Sheriff's evil Moloch spell of deception and fear. We do not have much time left. Believe in the miracles you were about to witness!"

While people kneeled, bowing their heads, Anthony discarded his old shoes and ran barefoot up to the pulpit. He snatched up the smoldering Nikes.

"Put those evil shoes down!" Angela shouted.

Smiling, he quickly put them on his bare feet, and they fit like a glove. The feel of his feet wrapped in the fine, warm soft cotton padding was more comfortable than he could had ever imagined.

"These shoes ain't ever coming off my feet!" he mumbled softly. He looked around to see the entire congregation silently staring at him in horror. Others shook their heads in disbelief and prayed for him. More members left, putting as much distance as they could between Anthony, those shoes and the church.

Jeremiah warned him. "Anthony, those shoes ain't going to bring you nothing but trouble, take them off like she said, boy!"

He waved Jeremiah off.

"You must be out of your mind! Are you crazy?" He turned back to the crowd, pointing his thumb mockingly at Jeremiah. "He must still be under that witch's spell!"

Anthony could not care less about the warnings. As an afterthought, he checked his pants pocket for his twenty-seven cents . . . . *and I still made me some cash.* He knelt down to figure out what to do with the double pair of shoestrings. At that moment, his mother Josephine burst into the entrance at the back of the church.

"What's going on in here? Where is my boy, Anthony?" She looked around. "I just saw Carolyn run by me scared as a jack rabbit, dragging her two little chilluns home. She told me my boy Anthony was in here and some crazy stuff was going on." She pushed through the crowd. Trailing right behind her were Anthony's seven brothers and sisters.

Hearing his mothers' angry voice, Anthony froze, remembering the groceries taken by the deputies. *Big Momma is going to kill me about those groceries!* He got busy tying tight knots in his shoestrings.

A woman standing next to Big Momma spoke up. "He's up there by the pulpit, Josephine! He's up in the front, bent down and he's got on them demon shoes!"

"He got on demon shoes? What in the name of God are you talking about?" She marched through the crowd.

"Anthony … Anthony, where are you, boy?"

The crowd of silent parishioners suddenly opened for Josephine like the parting of the Red Sea.

"Anthony? What you doing down there and where's your coat at? Boy, you better be praying!" She stormed toward him, fuming, afraid and relieved all at the same time. His brothers and sisters followed directly behind her. They all wore smug smirks, happy to see he was in trouble with their scolding mother. Her approach was like that of a lioness. "Boy, you better speak up quick! Where you been? You got these kids and me out here running around through the cold dark woods looking for you. Don't be shining me on, boy, you better speak up cause I'm 'bout ready to whip the blackness off your hide right here in church in front of everybody!"

Anthony, still kneeling with his back turned, did not move a muscle.

"Where are my groceries? You had me sick disappearing like that worrying about you being snatched or eaten up by something! You had better answer me, boy! I asked you where is your coat and my groceries at, Anthony? Don't you hear me talking to you? I said where you been?" She demanded, getting angrier at his insolence. Anthony stood up, facing her. She gasped seeing his bloody, beaten face. She removed the blanket and moaned in grief turning him in a circle, seeing the bleeding whipped welts that covered his body. She tried to hug him, causing him to scream. Her tone of voice changed to pity and angry sorrow.

"Oh, my poor baby, who put a whip to you? What was going on round here, Reverend? Who's put the whip on my boy?" Her face wore a thunderous look as she scanned the crowd.

"It was the sheriff's men, Momma. He is on his way back here and he is going to kill everybody if them strangers aren't turned over to him!"

She looked sternly to the reverend, noticing the newcomers standing close.

"You don't understand what's been happening here tonight, Josephine!" The reverend attempted to explain. Her arm around her son got terribly hot. She felt the boy's head.

"Somebody get me a cold towel for my boy, he's burning up with fever. Somebody better start talking to me about what is going on around here!"

Deacon Phillips fetched her the towel. She looked directly at him.

"Well, Deacon?" she asked.

The deacon silently pointed down at her son's feet. She stepped back to get a better look at the strange white shoes her boy was wearing.

"Them ain't your shoes, boy. Where you get them from? Did you steal them? Is that why the sheriff took a whipping to you? You take them off right this second! Take 'em off right now, I say." She turned to the reverend. "Reverend Bishop, please, what is going on here?" Before the good reverend could say or do anything, Anthony cried out.

"Help me, Momma!" The shoes had burst into flames. He hollered trying to pull them off, but they were knotted to his feet. His entire body became totally consumed in fire; he screamed in sheer terror and agony.

Stepping away from him in horror, she dropped the wet towel to the floor. "No, no, not my boy! Do something! Someone! My baby! Aaanthoneeeeeeeee!"

His flaming arms fling about trying to reach out for her. "MOMMA?" Seconds later, his burnt body crumbled to the floor in a pile of gray ashes.

Well, as far as most of the congregation was concerned, that pretty much covered it for the evening as far as witnessing miracles. All hell broke loose again. People did not know what to believe at this point. In the midst of the chaos, Anthony's mother dropped to her knees on the floor, sobbing. Her arms outstretched in agony, she screamed in horror shaking balled fists full of ashes up to the ceiling.

"Why, Lord? Why?" Her children surrounded her, screaming and crying, clinging on to her.

Anthony's brother, Eddie-Lee, caught a glimmer of silver twinkling from the pile of Anthony's ashes. He knelt down as if in prayer and slyly scooped up a handful of ash and the twenty-seven cents. Feeling the three warm coins, he slipped the handful of ash quietly into his pocket. His mother looked up to see the reverend had returned to the pulpit with Jeremiah. She looked at them in grief and terror. She wept pitifully, letting his ashes spill out of her hands.

"WHAT IN THE NAME OF GOD IS HAPPENING IN THIS CHURCH? What in the hell is going on here? He was a good boy ... he didn't deserve to die like that, Reverend!"

Not waiting on a response, Josephine shouted to them all, "This is a Church of Black Evilness!" She gathered her children and left.

Hope and Angela walked up to the pulpit together armed with their golden swords. They raised their weapons. Hope took hold of Angela's hand as the blue aura reappeared around them.

"Let them realize their true purpose! Let us be strong for our battle begins now!"

The faithful elders, along with all the orphans and children, saw the truth immediately. Mr. Leotis, along with some others, marveled at what was occuring.

All looked up in awe, however, as the bright pale blue aurora swirled around inside the large church. Angela and Hope began to sing, their beautiful voices louder and louder with each verse. Those men and women chosen to do battle transformed into warriors dressed in golden armor. In each of their hands appeared a golden shield, trimmed in silver and inlaid with a silver cross. In their other hands materialized a golden weapon chosen just for them. They looked at each other in astonishment. Others not in battle dress now appeared in black monk's robes. They awaited further instructions.

Angela stood proudly in front of them. She raised her two gleaming swords of gold smiled at the small army of gallant warriors. They totaled two hundred and fifteen.

"We fight not against the County Sheriff Ezekiel Joppa, but Ezekiel Joppa, the evil leader of the Moloch clan. He commands the evil souls brought to fight against us in this battle. Believe! Stand up for righteousness and your faith. Now comes the time we must go to war to fight and keep hope and our future alive. Fear not—if faced with the ultimate sacrifice of death, for you will have fulfilled your purpose. We do not face death, but Heaven and everlasting life as your reward for standing against evil this day!"

Everyone raised their weapons with shouts of praise for victory. She proudly crossed her swords above her head.

Angela turned as Jeremiah walked up by her side. He looked magnificent in his battle dress of silver and gold armor, with matching ax and shield. She smiled at the two thick plumes, one red and one blue, that hung from the top of his helmet. He smiled.

"I am here to stand beside you in battle as you stood with me, my love."

Angela made a confession. "I knew of you and fell in love long after this day we met. I come from the future, Jeremiah! I understand now that I am your guardian angel that stood and fought beside you." She tenderly placed her hand on his breastplate over his heart.

"You are my dream come true, just as I am yours. I dreamed of you in my mortal life in the twenty-first century. You came and captured my heart over a hundred and forty in the years in the future. You are my guy … That Guy!"

Her confession brought everything to light. Overwhelmed with joy, he turned to Hope, shouting, "Hey, that's right! I'm that guy! It truly was Angela, my guardian angel. That was what she used to call me in my dreams! Hey, y'all.... I'M THAT GUY!"

CHAPTER 21

Faith Is With Me

While Jeremiah was having ecstatic realizations, the Reverend James Bishop in present-day Mariah was terribly upset, having no success in trying to get in touch with John. No one had seen or heard from him. He was more concerned about the whereabouts of his holy altar cross, which John had in his possession. The phone rang. He reached for the receiver, then hesitated, pulling a handkerchief from his pocket. Covering it, he held it up away from his ear, making sure there were no strange and painful buzzing sounds at the other end.

"Hello?" He finally spoke.

"Have you held true to your word?" It was the Moloch, Helen Troy. Her sultry voice spoke through the phone.

"Thank God it's you. Yes, yes! I have spoken to no one of our conversation. "What was the price you asked in exchange for the relic you possess?"

"Just bring Faith with you," she parried. "I seek reclamation, same as you! I need you to bring me Faith and help put an end to all this madness!"

"Just bring faith with me?" the reverend asked.

"Yes, bring Faith!" the woman repeated.

"Is that all?"

"Yes. All I need you to do is to have Faith with you when we meet. I have the relic. "

"Well, that's no problem. Where are we to meet?" The reverend asked, picking up his Bible.

"We will meet at the site of your church, where else? I will see you there in exactly one hour!" the woman demanded.

"Yes, yes, that's perfect. No one should be around then," the tipsy reverend replied, looking at his watch.

"One hour," she said. The phone went dead.

The reverend wiped off the receiver and nervously pat his sweating forehead. He finished his glass of sherry and went to the closet for his hat and coat. He stopped at the table and filled a large flask. On his way out, he had just one more drink of encouragement. He walked out the front door, remembering the woman's main request that he bring faith with him.

"Oops! I almost forgot!" He returned into the house and came back out with his bible. He had his own plan to stop what was going on. If he was going to meet with this evil whatever she was he needed the gift from God, the church altar cross. In one last desperate attempt, he decided to stop by John's house.

Pulling up in front, he looked at himself in the rear view mirror and put on his sunglasses. He was about to knock when he saw a note stuck in the screen door. Ringing the doorbell, there was no answer. He banged heavily on the door.

"John, John Davidson … it's Reverend Bishop." The sky above rumbled, producing a loud thunderclap.

Still getting no answer, he checked the time on his watch. With much trepidation, he turned away to leave. The front door opened.

"Reverend Bishop? Is that you?"

Elated at hearing John's voice, he turned to see him.

"Thank you, Lord. Thank you, Jesus!" The reverend raised his arms up and ran over to John. He grabbed and hugged him tightly, overjoyed.

"Thank God you're here, John! My prayers have been answered! I have been desperately trying to reach you all day. I need my cross! Where in heaven's name have you been? Everyone's been worried sick about you...." Smelling smoke, the reverend looked down.

"John, why are your socks smoking like that, son?"

John looked down at his smoldering socks, wondering what happened to his Nikes. "It's a long story. I have so much to tell you. Please, please come in, Reverend, I have so much to share with you about what is happening.' John paused to get his bearings straight, still a little dazed from his time traveling *miracle*. With a weird, puzzled look, he focused on the reverend.

"What's happened to your face?" John asked. The reverend looked sick, his face bloated. His skin looked dead. The smell of wine easily overwhelmed the Old Spice he overused trying to mask his drunkenness.

"As you know and can see I haven't been well lately, John." The reverend attempted to gain some sympathy, quickly hiding his blistering hands behind his back.

John went on to explain the miraculous return of Hope and Angela and their journey back to the year 1867. He spoke gravely, relating all the details of his time in the past and the two battles about to take place there and in the present.

John's babbling rant was too much for the intoxicated reverend to comprehend or believe. His eyes got tight with scrutiny and suspicion. The tipsy reverend stopped John.

"What have you been doing in here? Why are your feet smoking and smelling like that?" The reverend sniffed the air again, getting a faint whiff of sulfur.

"Are you high, son? Have you been smoking something in here? Where is my cross, son?"

"No, no, I ain't been smoking anything, Reverend Bishop! You know I don't mess around like that!"

"John, listen to me, I—I have to be somewhere and—I don't have the time to figure all this out! I have to be where I am going in less than twenty minutes. Our battle has already started and I need my cross! We already know the evil has returned to Mariah. They tried an attack inside Rosemary's home attempting to kidnap Faith, John."

"What did you say … attacked? What has been going on around here, Reverend?"

"Everyone's looking for you. I just talked to Rosemary. We never had such a bold attempt by them to cross over like this before, John. That is where you should be heading right now, son! Go protect them until I get there! Now give me my cross!" he demanded.

"Is Faith all right? Did any harm come to her?"

The reverend began to realize John was avoiding handing over the cross.

"Yes, yes, Faith is fine John I just don't have the time to explain it all right now! Just give me my altar cross and get yourself over to the Matthews'! They want you there with them."

John stood motionless, feeling the Reverend's angry glare coming from behind his sunglasses. The reverend had had his fill of John's games.

"The cross, damn it, John, I need you to give it to me right now!" He boldly began walking through John's house searching for the cross. John followed right behind him.

"That's what I was about to tell you, Reverend," John responded glumly.

"Where is my cross, damn you!" He cursed again. He turned and grabbed John by his shoulders, shaking him violently. "Just give me my cross, boy!"

"Hey man, take your hands off me! What is up with you? Hold on a minute!" John pulled from the Reverend's grasp and backed away.

"I will not accept any more delay on this matter, John. Give me my cross, now!"

"Okay ... okay ... check this out, Reverend ... I do not have it to give to you. I left it back in Mariah."

"Well, come on, let's go to town and get it!" The reverend hurried toward the door.

"We can't!" John responded.

"What do you mean, we can't?"

"I'm saying we can't! It is in Mariah, but it is not here in *this* Mariah.

"What are you talking about, John?" the reverend asked, perplexed.

"We can't get it because I left it back in the year 1867! I left it there to protect Hope, Angela and the child, Easter. That is what I have been trying to tell you all this time! We traveled back to 1867 Mariah in order to keep the child from capture by the Moloch. I know it is hard to believe, but I gave the Holy Cross to your great, great grandfather Joshua as a gift from God. They are getting ready to fight in a spiritual battle in Mariah's past right at this very moment!"

"Are you sure you are not just waking up from some strange nightmare? All of us are having visions lately, son," the Reverend asked, doubting John's audacious story.

"Nope it is like I said, I was just sent back here, the cross is not here, and we can't go get it! And, I left a brand new pair of two-hundred-dollar Air Jordans back there, too!"

"My God, son, are you sure you're all right?" *Boy, you done gone and went all the way plain crazy! I knew it would be just a matter of time before you totally snapped! You never did get over tripping about the death of your parents!* He looked at his watch. He only had fifteen minutes left to get to the church site.

"Please, John, just do what I say and go be with Rosemary and Faith, they need you there now. I got to go and if I were you I would stop inhaling that smoke coming out your socks there!" He wiped his sweaty brow with his coat sleeve.

"But, Reverend Bishop, I've got to tell you…!" The reverend dismissed John, cutting him off. John followed him to the front door to explain further. "Reverend Bishop, the battle—"

"John, I know of the coming battle and the return of the evil priestess. Because of you we have to go into battle without the Gift from God to help defend us!"

Tell Rosemary that we have talked and that we no longer possess the gift. I will join you all shortly and explain everything to everyone when I get there. I have to go!" Looking at his watch again, he rushed out the door.

"What day is it today?" John asked.

"Jesus, John, its Christmas! God be with you, son," he hollered and jumped into his car, not bothering to look back.

"And may He be with you, too, Reverend Bishop."

Sadly closing his front door, he saw the folded note stuck in the screen door. Faith had left it there, stopping by an hour after he began his journey with Faith and Angela. He pulled it out and read:

> John I am so worried about you! Where are you? Christmas is in two days! Please come over to Momma's as soon as you read this! We desperately need you here with us! I feel something terrible is among us.
>
> Your loving fiancée,
> Faith

John rushed to his room to put on a clean pair of socks and another pair of shoes.

* * *

A heavy night fog rolled down as dusk settled over the valley. Helen Troy sat in her black Chevy pickup, impatiently waiting on the reverend's arrival while her twins sat quietly in the back in their car seats. They had grown quite a bit since the start of the battle.

"Soon as he shows up with Faith, we will have all that is needed!"

Helen balled her fist tightly and burst into laughter. The babies held up their hands and gave each other little high-fives. Looking deeply into their eyes, she made them a promise. "As for the good reverend, his will be the first heart you will taste, marinated heavily in a sweet mixture of sin and religion. You will drink his hot blood and, believe me, you will enjoy every morsel of him as if it were . . . mmmm, Heaven sent." She began to laugh again and the twins joined her by pounding on their car seats, screaming in delight.

The lights of the reverend's car approached out of the mist, pulling up to the church. The children became silent. Helen's eyes turned red with rage at seeing him arrive alone.

The Reverend stumbled around the construction site with his bible in hand. He looked at the nearly completed church with a frown.

"Hellooo, is anyone around? Yooohoooo, I'm exactly on time!" he called out. He staggered around in a nervous drunken stupor, having finishing off his flask on the way there. Holding his bible tightly against his chest, he called out again. "I've brought faith, as you asked! I can hear your confessions. We can pray together and ask for forgiveness and seek your redemption."

Unseen by him, Helen watched his every intoxicated move. "Oh no, he didn't, why that stupid drunken ... idiot!" she shouted angrily.

"Idd--jit!" the frowning twins whispered, mimicking their mother, shaking their heads in dissatisfaction.

The baby Patience whispered, "Me humgry, Mommy!" Helen turned to her babies and placed a finger to her lips for them to be quiet.

"I know, baby, Mommy will bring you back something to eat real soon. Just give me a minute. I'll be right back," Helen purred in a low voice. She blew them both a kiss and disappeared.

Reverend Bishop, standing at the bottom of the steps of the church, nervously observed the front door slowly open. Out stepped Helen, holding the wooden chest in her hands. She was quite disturbed as she looked around.

"You came here alone, preacher man?" Her fine-looking face was familiar, but he could not place it.

"Yes! Don't I know you from somewhere, young lady?" he asked.

Ignoring his question, Helen replied, "I told you to bring Faith."

The tipsy reverend patted his bible. "Faith is right here with me."

The indignation smeared on her face made him shiver.

"Well, where the hell is she?" Helen demanded angrily. "I hope for your sake you have her locked up in the trunk!"

"Who?" he fearfully asked.

"Faith Matthews!" she bitterly spat back at him.

The reverend ridiculously tried to play innocent, knowing well the mistake he has made.

"Faith Matthews?"

"Who else, fool?"

"You asked me to bring faith with me." He showed his bible again, causing Helen to laugh hilariously.

"Ha-ha.... What? Why, you drunken idiot, did I say bring YOUR faith. I was talking about Faith Matthews, the twin, you alcoholic imbecilic fool." She held up the box for him to see.

"I have fulfilled my part of the bargain. I have brought what you seek as promised. We cannot proceed any further until you bring to me what I asked of you. Now, go and get Faith Matthews and bring her back here to me!"

"What evil are you?" The reverend asked.

She wanted terribly to kill him right there on the spot. He backed away as Helen put him in a trance. She opened the chest and held up the beautiful, ancient mask. Reverend Bishop was unable to turn his eyes away. Helen slowly moved the sinister mask closer and closer to his face until the reverend could no longer resist the urge. He dropped his bible, grabbing hold of the mask, kissing it passionately, turning him into pure evil. She yanked the mask away.

As promised, they would dine on the pathetic man's heart. Her babies, ravenously hungry, wanted to feed. However, they would have to wait just a wee bit longer. His services were still needed to go fetch Faith Matthews.

"We will toast this union with a glass of sherry." She coaxed the reverend with two silver goblets that magically appeared in her hands. His parched throat felt like sand paper.

"Yes, yes." He licked his lips. He greedily gulped down the wine. He looked up into the foggy night sky, his eyes glowing grey. He was one of them ... a Moloch. "I see it all clearly now. Faith is a sacrifice that has to be made. Faith must be vanquished for us to prevail today. I will bring her to you as you command, my lady!" He obsequiously obeyed.

He got in his car and drove straight to Rosemary's house.

Chapter 22

Here I Come To Save the Day

Having ten o'clock tea, the Matthews quietly sat around the dining room table. Faith was next to her mother, recovering, wearing a nightgown and still feeling a little dazed. Rosemary was about to speak when a loud heavy knock pounded at the front door.

"Who's that banging on my door like that?" Rosemary loudly snapped. Not wanting to leave Faith alone she asked, "Someone please answer that door for me."

"I'll get it," Esther insisted, getting up.

"Be careful opening that door, sister. You know our battle has already begun!"

"Amen to that!" Esther shouted back as she cautiously walked down the hallway to the front door. Another loud, impatient knock sounded on the door.

"I'm coming, hold your horses! Who is it?"

No one answered. She mumbled to herself. "They knock like they the police or something." Standing on her tiptoes, she peeked from behind pulled curtains covering the door's arched window. Seeing no one there, she turned and shouted back to the others.

"There's no one out here!"

She turned to the window, looking into the face of a man standing outside. His sudden appearance scared the wits out of her. Screaming, she jumped, grabbing her chest.

Hearing the commotion, Ruth shouted, "Esther what's wrong up there?" She grabbed her butt in pain.

John attempted to make apologies through the door.

"Oops, ma'am, I am so sorry about that ... I'm John, John Davidson! I didn't mean to scare you."

Catching her breath, she opened the door, plenty perturbed. She hollered back to the others, "I'm okay! It's that boy, John!" She greeted him with an angry scowl. She did not care much for John's playful little ruse. Esther mumbled resentfully under her breath as he attempted to give her a better first impression.

"I'm Faith's fiancé, John Davidson. I was expecting Faith to answer the door. I wanted to surprise her." He gave her a broad smile, holding out his hand.

Hearing his voice, Faith jumped out of her seat.

"John's back! It's John, Momma!" Running down the hallway, she rushed past Esther into his arms, kissing and hugging him tightly. Ruth let out a grunt of disappointment, seeing Faith's underclothing through the nightgown as they embraced. Faith stepped back to take a good look at him.

"Girl, you show Auntie some respect. Now go get some proper clothes on."

"Sorry, Auntie! I will go put something on right now."
She turned to John. "Give me a minute to change, okay?
So much has happened and I have so much to tell you and
I'm so glad you're back!"

Meanwhile, Esther was closely scrutinizing John.
Faith introduced them.

"Aunt Esther, this is John! John, this is my Aunt
Esther!" She bragged joyously, patting him lovingly on
the chest. She kissed him on the cheek and ran out of the
room to get dressed.

"Well, well, the boy lost has finally returned home.
Oh, I know who you are! You are a little old to be playing
them kind of games at people's front doors like that, son.
You know you could have given me a heart attack! I could
have dropped dead right here! What would you have done
then? How do ... I'm Rosemary's sister, Esther," she said
uncomfortably. She lightly shook his outstretched hand.
Their touching made her nose twitch.

"A Merry Christmas to you! I've heard so much about
you and your sister, Ruth," John acknowledged, pulling
off his coat and rubbing his hands together to get warm.
"Man, has it gotten cold out there tonight!"

"God bless and Merry Christmas!" she told him,
giving him a cold, uneasy stare and placing his coat and
hat on the rack.

Easter walked ahead of him into kitchen. As they
entered, she rolled her eyes at her sisters.

Rosemary was first to speak.

"John! Thank the Lord you are here, you can't imagine
what has been going on in this house lately. We got so

much to tell you. Just hours ago, an evil spirit came here with twin babies and attacked us. They tried to enter our world through a mirror upstairs. They tried to—"

Faith walked in. "John, where have you been? I have been worried sick and going crazy without you. Did you get the note I left on your door two days ago?"

"I just got your note, Faith, and came as soon as I saw it. Hello, Mrs. Matthews, I hope you and everybody are all right."

"We're all right, John. This is my other sister, Ruth."

"Pleased to meet you. John!" She shook his hand warmly. Her nose twitched, too, when she touched him.

"Thanks to my sisters, they won't be trying that little stunt again!" Rosemary replied, noticing her sisters' adverse reaction and apprehension.

"I guess we all are still a little stressed out from all the excitement that's been going on around here." She gave her sisters a look of concern.

"I have a lot to share with you, also!" John replied.

"I bet you do!" Ruth quipped.

Rosemary felt uncomfortable in his presence, the same as her sisters. There was great tension in the room Ruth leaned over to her sister and whispered.

"Something ain't right and he ain't all that ... righteous! I got to talk to you." They both agreed. Esther made a suggestion. "I've gotten a sudden chill. Would anyone besides me like some more hot tea?"

"Yes, good idea, Esther, and let's take it in the dining room. I'll come help get the table ready!"

Rosemary rolled her eyes at her sisters as they left the room. Esther scrutinized John with a shady look before walking out. Ruth whispered to Esther, "Something just ain't kosher about that boy."

"You ain't got to tell me! He is full of himself and full of it! I tell you I could have sworn I smelled something bad when he walked by me in the hallway. I can't put my finger on it but he smells...."

"Tainted? I smelled it, too!" Her sister nailed it.

Meanwhile, in the kitchen, John began telling his story to Faith and Rosemary.

"You must believe what I am about to tell you because it is all so incredible! I have just returned from a journey back to the year 1867 Hope and Angela, you know, Sheriff Solomon."

Rosemary immediately lit up hearing Hope's name.

"You have been with Hope in the year 1867? How can that be possible, John? Come sit next to me and explain how you could be with my baby over a century ago, and you mentioned she was with Angela Solomon?"

"Sounds impossible, huh?" John replied. Concerned, she took his hand into hers.

"Yeah, umm . . . I just saw Reverend Bishop before I left home to come over here. He was trying to explain something to me about of all kinds of stuff going on. How everyone has been having strange visions and you guys being attacked here. Talking about strange, he was acting all weird himself, Rosemary! He had been drinking, too! He was walking all around my house talking crazy, getting mad at me all up in my face. He told me to tell you that he had some kind of important meeting to go to but he will meet with us here later." He paused.

"Oh yeah ... we don't have the gift from God, either."

"Maybe it would be better if you explain everything from the very beginning," Rosemary said. "First, I want to hear all about Hope's return."

John explained everything about their return in order to save and protect the child, Easter. He soon had them sitting on edge as he spun tales of his journey over the past forty-eight hours. The sisters gasped hearing how they avoided capture by the Moloch in the woods nearby by transporting miraculously through time.

They listened as John went on to explain how Sheriff Angela Solomon had fallen in love with a man in the past named Jeremiah. Their feelings turned to displeasure hearing how the people living in Mariah turned against them and how they were on the run for their lives from Ezekiel Joppa, Mariah's county sheriff. He ended his testimony warning of the two coming battles.

"Both battles are about to take place, and we must be victorious!" He paused to let it all sink in.

Rosemary sat quietly, her attention focusing back and forth between listening to John and thinking of Hope's perilous dilemmas taking place in the past. Hope's voice whispered in her ear. Upon receiving the sudden revelation, Rosemary immediately interrupted.

"John, don't you have more to tell us?"

"Yes! Yes, I do," John humbly responded. He turned to Faith, taking her hand into his own.

"I ask for your forgiveness, Faith. While I was with Hope, I realized how much I missed and loved her. I could not help myself. Heck! I thought I was going to live the rest of my life back there in the past! I confess I hold love in my heart for the both of you, a love that still hounds me. Please, I ask you to forgive me for the infidelity of loving you both." John looked despondently at Faith with big puppy dog eyes. Faith sat in silence as tears clouded her eyes. She always knew of and feared his love for her sister. Rosemary knew that John had not confessed all that he should, as did Faith. Rosemary was about to speak on this when a loud banging knock came from the front door again. Ruth and Esther turned anxiously. The heavy thumps put John on edge; it reminded him of Sheriff Joppa pounding at the front door of Seth and Mattie's general store. Rosemary got up.

"I'll answer this one!" Walking in a manly manner down the hallway to the front door, Rosemary shouted with attitude. "I know my doorbell is working! There is no reason for nobody to be banging on my door like that! Now who is that out there beating on my door?"

"Rosemary! It's me ... Reverend Bishop! Hurry up and open the door!"

Rosemary looked out the window and smiled. There was something odd about him, though. He looked like a secret agent with his hat pulled down low to his eyebrows, coat collar popped up and sunglasses on. She unlocked the door anyway.

He greeted her with a troubled grin and walked in. "Hello, Rosemary."

"Praise the Lord, Reverend Bishop, you finally made it! Let me take your coat and hat. What perfect timing. Come in, John is here!" She looked at him with nervous concern.

"No, that won't be necessary, I won't be staying long. I must see Faith!" He stumbled as he tried to step around Rosemary. Having stopped by the store to get his drink on again, the reverend gave off the smell of wine and Old Spice. She could not believe he had the nerve to walk into her house without taking off his hat, obviously inebriated. This was more than she could take and she was immediately sorry she'd opened the door so quickly.

"Hold it right there a minute, Reverend Bishop. Have you been drinking?"

He bowed his head and waved his hand over her mouth, clamping it shut and freezing her in place. She could not open her mouth to scream nor move from his spell. She could taste the smell of sulfur rising in the air.

CHAPTER 23

Confrontations

"Who is that, Momma?" Faith called out. Hearing her voice come from the back Reverend Bishop quickly moved down the hallway, leaving Rosemary standing at the front door in a frozen trance. He entered the dining room, arms raised in front of him. Pointing at Esther and Ruth, he mumbled a chant, paralyzing them both in their seats. John shouted, "Reverend Bishop ... stop! Stay away from him, Faith. I see what you are, Reverend!" The not-so-holy man spoke directly to Faith, paying no attention to John. "I have come for you, Faith, my child. We must leave now and go to church. I need you to come with me so we can prevail in the battle that is about to take place. We have no time to lose. We must leave now!" He opened his arms and walked toward her like a zombie. She tried to back away, but could not move a muscle. John thrust himself front of Faith to protect her.

The reverend growled at them like a wild animal. He waved his arm, releasing a powerful force that knocked John up against the wall, placing him under a binding spell. John struggled, unable to move. Everything around him moved in slow motion. The heavy gagging smell of sulfur mixed with wine and Old Spice filled the air.

"Come, we must save the day, my angel!" Reverend Bishop grabbed Faith.

"My Faith is not going anywhere with you, buster!" The reverend was whacked from behind, upside the back of his head. Dazed by the blow, he turned around, cringing in pain. Rosemary stood behind him, firmly gripping a heavy, black cast iron skillet in both of her hands. "She is staying right here with me!" Rosemary swung again, smacking it squarely against the right side of the reverend's face, busting it open. He fell to his knees. "And *this* is for bringing evil into my house, and being drunk and not taking off your hat!" She reared back with the heavy iron pan. The last powerful blow broke his nose, knocking off his hat and sunglasses. Rosemary saw that his fluttering, dazed eyes were no longer brown but bloodshot grey, like the Moloch. He crashed to the floor in a dead heap.

Instantly the others snap out of the evil trances placed upon them.

"He was one of them," John said, getting up off the floor and rubbing the back of his head. "Nice work, Mrs. Matthews! Dang! We all must go to the church now—that is where he was going to take Faith!"

"Us too?" Esther questioned.

"Yes, everyone!" John answered.

"Just wait one minute, I must go upstairs and get something!" Rosemary responded, rushing herself up to her room. She retreated into her room and everything went white. She collapsed on the bed. Minutes passed while the others waited, getting worried They were about to check on her when she stepped out. She had two bibles given to her daughters by John and something wrapped in a blanket. There was something different about her.

"Are you all right, Momma?" Faith asked.

"I am fine, child." She replied, in a serene state of mind.

"What about Reverend Bishop?" Faith asked as she stepped around him laid out on the floor.

John checked his pulse. "He is no longer with us."

"Good, leave him be. We got to go to the church now!" Rosemary answered. She briskly walked out the door, leaving without looking back.

"Is that our Reverend Bishop's grandson?' Ruth questioned.

Frightened, Esther turns to her sister.

"It sure is! I told you we shouldn't a come back here; you can't even trust your own preacher these days!"

"Let's go!" Esther replied, pulling her along.

On their way to the church, Rosemary told them to prepare themselves.

"I am glad we will all stand together to face this challenge."

"And we suppose to fight this evil in hand to hand combat with no weapons, no protection?" Esther sarcastically grumbled.

"You have already battled on faith alone upstairs, sister!" Rosemary reminded her, handing the bibles to her sisters.

"Yeah, we did!" Ruth proudly confirmed.

"Yep, we sure did! Thank you, Jesus!" Esther praised.

The five got in the car and drove over to the church.

Sitting in a lotus position and chanting in a trance, the Moloch Helen awaited the reverend's return. She was chanting, rocking back and forth, as John and the Matthews family drove up. A mist rose in the woods. Rosemary turned around and warned everyone.

"Stay in the car. Do not leave the car until I motion for you to come forward!"

"No, mother, it is I that needs to confront her! Her evil is strong and powerful. She will kill you!" Faith said bravely.

"No, my child, I have been told what must be done here. Just do as I say!" Rosemary firmly commanded as she got out of the car.

"I'm coming!" John attempted to follow. She leaned her body against his door keeping it shut. "No, John, you most of all must stay here and protect Faith and my sisters. Just stay in the car until I am done with what I got to do. You will soon see!" Rosemary slowly walked toward Helen. She unwrapped the blanket, unveiling the golden ram horn she carried with her. Helen stopped chanting and floated just off the ground to confront her adversary.

"So, I see the reverend has greatly surpassed all my expectations this time. Somehow, that drunken fool has managed to bring the entire Matthews clan to me. Where is my good fellow? I owe the good reverend a great deal of pleasure," Helen declared, floating by Rosemary.

"He is no longer with us as he has fallen by my hand. You do know who I am, evil one?" Rosemary responded defiantly.

"So it was by your hand!" Ignoring the question, Helen smiled.

"You really don't know who I am, do you?" Rosemary challenged again.

"Of course, I know who you are, Rosemary Matthews! But it really doesn't matter now, since I see Faith and the boy John Davidson and your two sisters here with you."

Rosemary paid no attention to the statements and proclaimed, "I come as your executioner and to save you from a fate worse than death itself, my child! This will be your last day here on earth."

"Wow, now that's pretty scary!" Helen mocked. She smiled and snapped her fingers, creating a loud thunderclap. Dark clouds began forming over the clearing.

Rosemary looked to the darkened skies as Helen floated around her.

Back in the car, alarmed by both Helen floating around and the spectacle in the sky above, Esther said, "Look up in the sky, that flying witch is conjuring up something evil. I am not going to sit here and let my sister face all this alone." She opened the car door. "Me neither," Ruth said getting out of the car.

"Aunties, Momma told us to stay here!" Faith warned.

"Well, you best do what your Momma told you and stay in the car, child. That's my baby sister out there and I'm going to help her face that evil floating around!" Esther responded. John quickly sided with Esther and Ruth.

"You're right, Esther. Come on, Rosemary needs us!" John jumped out of the car.

Ruth and Esther trailed behind, praying, each holding a bible. They grabbed hold of their small metal crosses around their necks. They snatched them off, clinging tightly to them in the palms of their hands.

A blue shroud suddenly covered Faith's body as she changed into full golden battle armor. The two sisters now wore the black monk's robes. John doesn't change at all.

Rosemary was concentrating her focus on the confrontation with Helen. "I know of all your plans, Helen. There are no more secrets. The end you speak of will not be allowed to happen!"

Wearing a big grin, Helen acknowledged Faith's arrival as she and the others crossed the clearing.

"Well, well ... look-see what we got us here! Oooh, girlfriend, what a cute little golden outfit you have on!"

Rosemary turned. "I TOLE you all to STAY IN THE CAR!"

Helen saw John and crooned to him, "Bad boy, bad boy, what'cha' gonna do? What'cha gonna do when dey come for yoooou!"

John froze in his tracks at hearing her musical mockery.

"Well, it's about time you showed yourself, Boy Wonder! I've been looking all over for you. I heard you were back."

Rosemary grimaced as Faith walked by and stood toe to toe, staring straight into Helen's evil grey eyes. Neither showed any fear of the other. Helen slowly floated around her, giving Faith the once over.

"Honey you are just too cute!" Helen patronized the young woman's boldness.

Faith snapped. "You evil witch, I see you have returned to Mariah. Last time I saw you, you were running away with your tail between your legs. I would run away in shame, too, if I were the bearing the seed of my husband's father!"

Rosemary could not believe these two are going at it like a couple of envious, spiteful teenagers. She sternly interrupted the immature catfight, scolding her daughter for not obeying her commands.

"Faith, you were to stay in the car as I told you."

Faith ignored her mother's statement.

"Momma, I got this!" She loaded her bow. "We know you possess the mask. I am the one that has hunted you as you burned our holy places. We have been sent to put a final end to you, you evil wench, you unholy cow."

Helen returned a cold, deathly stare.

Rosemary turned in exasperation. "Lord, has everyone lost their minds around here? I warned all of you to stay in the car!"

Now standing beside her, Ruth snapped back, "What are you talking about? Do you see that?" She pointed up at the black swirling clouds above. "We were just coming to help you!"

Esther put the blame on John. "John told us you were in great danger and needed our help. Then we saw that thing up there appear!" She pointed to the black vortex. It was now twenty times the size it was before.

Rosemary looked up to see a swirling tunnel starting to open. She gave John a cold stare of betrayal.

"I should have known you were behind this!" She quickly turned her attention back to Helen, who was talking directly to Faith.

"We've been planning for your return since our first meeting almost a year and a half ago." Helen reminded Faith. "I told you then you were very special; today you will see why."

Rosemary desperately tried to attract Helen's attention.

"Your battle is not with her, Helen Troy, it is with me! Your time and life on this earth was a short evil one, but salvation can still be yours and even more importantly, you can save your twins. Yes, I know of your babies, Helen. You gave one of them my daughter's name of Hope and the other you named Patience. They are spawned from a seed of evil."

Helen was stunned, taken aback by the remark about her children. Faith was also surprised and infuriated.

"What? She got twins? Momma, those two evil babies in the mirror were hers? You mean to tell me that this witch named one of her evil daughters after my good sister, Hope?" She pulled her arrow taut in her golden bow.

Irritated, Rosemary pushed Faith's bow away and John stepped forward. "The chase is over, Church Burner. Give us the evil things you hide in your possession. Do as Rosemary says, witch."

Helen held a hand in John's face and rolled her eyes at him in disgust.

"Neeeegro, you of all people got your nerve! You should be on your knees begging for your own life, Boy Wonder, with all your little secrets!" She glared shrewdly at John.

"Shut up, Helen!" John shouted at her.

"Will you two let me handle this?" Rosemary pushed John and Faith behind her.

Helen looked up above and smiled. All the squabbling had given her the time she needed. She pointed toward the anomaly in the sky, shouting in the voice of Ezekiel Joppa.

"Come forth and take your righteous place here on earth and join us, my priestess, for as it has been spoken in time and on time, now your time has arrived. Let this be the world's darkest day!" She turned to the others pointing upward toward the black hole in the sky.

"Here comes someone that's dying to meet you all!"

A blood red cloud bellowed from within the center of the hole. Crackling lightning bolted and thunder flashed. The great hole bridged both time dimensions, revealing the same clearing where the Church of God stood back in 1867. In a flash, Helen appeared at the top of the stairs of the church, boasting, "Behold my father's plan!" She summoned forth her soldiers from hell.

A heavy rolling grey fog began to fill the clearing around the Matthews and John. The gray eyes of the Moloch began to multiply, as the whirling fog grew thicker. John shouted in panic.

"Faith! Help me! I need my armor for battle."

Faith grabbed the cross around her neck, praying as hard as she could. Nothing happened. She tapped him with her golden sword. A pale light covered John and he transformed; however, he was not dressed in the golden armor. The armor he wore was rusty and tainted.

Helen suddenly disappeared, appearing again behind Faith. She wrapped one arm around Faith's throat. In the other hand, she held a long dagger against Faith's neck.

"Let her go, evil one!" John warned Helen. He tried to draw his sword, but it stuck fast in its rusty sheath. Helen shouted back, laughing hysterically. "You fool! This was *my* father's plan from the very beginning. You all have fallen into our traps, in both worlds. We control the past, the present, and the now, the future. Where there is no Hope there is nothing, John, remember? So goes Faith, so goes the world! Isn't that right, Rosemary?"

CHAPTER 24

The Priestess Ilesha

Back in the past, camped in the woods surrounding the church, the Moloch made merry and feasted on those non-believers, captured when fleeing the church in fear. They served the young hearts of children captured to the sheriff on a silver platter. Piled high in front of him, he waved his hand over the organs, causing them to catch fire. He deeply breathed in the foul mixture of sulfur and burning flesh hanging heavily in the air around him. Watching the black clouds from above, he rocked slowly back and forth, chanting. He conjured up the Evil Priestess. The image rose out of the flames in the form of a fiery-coiled snake with the face of Ilesha Joppa. It slithered around the mound of burning hearts, eating a few, then coiled in front of him. Only he could see and hear her speak.

"Hello, Mother!" Sheriff Joppa greeted her in awe, as if still a child.

Taking human form and sitting next to him, she returned his greeting, bowing. She spoke sixteenth century English, coated with a heavy Eastern European accent.

"Hail to thee, my prince, my son! Tis been too long a time since thou hast last sat at my side!"

"Yes, Mother, it has been eons. I have missed you dearly!"

"I miss thee also, my son. You have done well to help make this our day. Now the moment nears to take back our destiny! So many battles have been fought here but none like the one that is about to begin. Two spiritual battles waged past and present, on the same battlefield, at the same moment. Battles that will determine the future destinies of everyone gathered."

She looked proudly at her son, rubbing his hair.

Sheriff Joppa laughed with joy listening to his mother bragging. He looked into her ghostly cold, transparent eyes as they feasted upon children's hearts.

Suddenly, the night sky exploded open. She pointed to the sky.

"You see, even as I speak I am summoned to the future. Look there, son!"

At the other end of the portal, they clearly saw the Church of God in the future. They observed Rosemary's confrontation, her arms outspread, with Helen floating around her on the church steps.

A flaming chariot drawn by four beastly creatures appeared in front of the opening to transport her through the portal. She rocketed through the sky, her flaming spirit landing on the back of the chariot. She screamed down to her son, grabbing hold of the bridle reins of fire. "Tis my time now, I beseech thee to be victorious this day, my son, for our plan must be perfect! Fare thee well, my prince, when next we meet I will be in the flesh and we shall celebrate our victory and rule the new worlds to be as IMMORTAL GODS! Take possession of the cross, make sacrifice of the infant, destroy and kill the ones from the future and everyone inside the Church. Leave nothing alive! Burn everything to the ground!"

Snapping her fingers, a long flaming whip of fire appeared in her hands. She cracked it down hard across the backs of the two hideous lead creatures. Her chariot whisked away into the whirling corridor of time with her screaming, "I'm coming, my dear, I'm coming!"

Her screams of liberation were heard on both sides of the portal and brought perverse joy to Joppa and Helen. The righteous ones, Hope in the past and Faith in the future, looked defiantly up toward the flaming vortex and simultaneously shouted, "Now, everyone!"

"Toll the bell, Reverend," Hope instructed. "Let our judgments begin." They both turned, hearing little hands tap against the heavy wooden church doors, this time followed by the small whimpering cries of a child.

"Open the door! Help me. Please!" The terrorized voice of a young boy begs from outside the door. "Somebody, please, please open the door! It's me, Eddie-Lee! Let me in! They ate my momma and killed by brothers and sisters!"

Hope warned, "We know not if it is a deception that knocks against that door. You have blessed this holy ground and evil can only breach these sanctified walls by the invitation of a holy man!"

The Reverend responded by walking up to the church doors.

"I cannot risk it. I It may truly be Josephine's child out there. No, no I will not bear the burden on my soul that I left her child standing out there alone, not after witnessing Anthony burn to ashes right in front of my own eyes!"

Mad barking dogs charge into the clearing. The door pounds frantically again.

"I do not know what stands on the other side of that door besides evil." Hope gave a final warning.

He unlocked and cracked the door ever so slightly. He saw Eddie-Lee on his knees, crying with his hands covering his face awaiting his approaching death.

"Get in here!" He snatched the child and flung him inside the church doors.

"Thank you, Jesus ... it's Josephine's boy, Eddie Lee!" As the boy slid across the wooden church floor, silver coins flew out of both his pockets.

The Reverend Bishop slammed shut the big church doors as the rabid dogs crashed into them against the door. He bolted the doors shut. Outside, the snarling dogs' razor sharp claws scratched wildly against them.

Everyone watched the boy crawl on his knees, greedily picking up his coins and stuffing them back in his pockets while crying about his mother and siblings.

The sounds of the dogs had gone silent. Gathering up all his coins, he sniveled, "It was horrible, horrible ... they ate my momma! They ate her alive and tore her apart. Then the sheriff's men killed all my brothers and sisters and cut out their hearts. My whole family is dead, Reverend!" The Reverend walked over and placed his hand on top of the boy's woolly head. He closed his eyes to pray for the boy and his lost family.

Eddie-Lee pulled his head away and snapped at the reverend's proffered hand. He was the Moloch invited into their safe refuge by a holy man; he had breached their sanctuary. He uncovered his face, revealing his evil grey eyes. Eddie-Lee bolted to the doors of the church, unlocking and swinging the big church doors wide open.

"Come, my friends . . . the good reverend has invited us in to dine! Dessert is now being served!" Eddie-Lee waved to the rest of the ghoulish horde, waiting outside in the clearing. Immediately the vicious dogs rushed in, on the attack. He laughed an evil little laugh. The boy turned and faced the reverend, exposing his grey eyes, and now a mouth full of fangs. He leapt toward the startled reverend and was immediately snatched out of the air by one of the giant wild dogs and swallowed whole.

Jeremiah and Angela led their own attack against the huge rabid hounds, charging through the aisles. Other righteous warriors joined with the reverend to help fight the beasts and try to close the doors of the church. Hope and her righteous brigade were engaged in frantic battle as the first horde of Moloch soldiers now spilled into the church. They were hideous demons of all sizes, all shapes—, the one thing they shared was that their snapping jaws dripped with gore and the blood of innocents.

The fighting thickened with them leaping over pews, plowing into the righteous and increasing in number. They picked up the scent of the child, Easter, who was hidden beneath the altar podium, and directed their attack toward it.

"The reverend must toll the bell, Jeremiah!" Angela warned as they fought the advancing horde of demons, their backs to the podium.

Heeding her warning, Jeremiah spun his axe like a buzz saw, mowing down the Moloch soldiers and giant beasts surrounding them like tree saplings. He looked over to Angela, fighting at his side, amazed by her prowess and strength, taunting her attackers. As she beheaded another beastly wolf creature, she proudly proclaimed, "Where be your master now? Show yourself to me and do battle, Ezekiel! Show yourself to me, cowardly one! Come confront your executioner! Sheriff Ezekiel Joppa! Show your true face! Confront me! I challenge you!"

There was an explosion at the front of the church. Answering her challenge, Sheriff Joppa appeared in a new demonic form.

"What female dares to challenge, to do battle against me?" his voice thundered. He was a huge, half-human Cyclops beast, his one eye glowing red and grey and bits of scraggly beard hanging from a chin as cloven as his demon feet. Black armor covered his huge bulging physique. A large, red five-pointed star shone from his breastplate and the front of his black horned helmet. He carried two curved black swords in each hand.

"Not only comes a woman, I am your executioner as well!"

Furious at her threat, he charged into the melee toward her with the force of a raving mad rhinoceros. He moved toward her, killing, knocking and tossing anyone in his path out of his way. The ground underneath his hoofed feet trembled.

Jeremiah suddenly leapt fearlessly in front of him and challenged, "You killed my Aunt Mattie and Uncle Seth. Your guise does not scare me, you evil . . . whatever you are! I seek my justice upon you for your evil deed against them!"

The sheriff-turned-beast stared furiously at Jeremiah as he continued with his challenge.

"I, Jeremiah Stone, challenge you, you ugly beast, and you shall fall!" He swung his mighty axe down hard upon the beast.

Crossing his swords, the sheriff easily thwarted Jeremiah's powerful blow. The beast bellowed a fierce prehistoric roar into Jeremiah's face.

"You dare stand against me, puny human? Get out of my way!" Ezekiel's swords penetrate through Jeremiah's armor like tinfoil. Stabbing Jeremiah in both sides, he impaled him above the ground.

"Nooooo!" Angela screamed in agony. The beast flung the warrior through the air. His body landed in front of Angela. He still lived, holding on to his axe and shield. Angela fell to her knees next to him, her weeping face stricken with grief and sorrow. The righteous ones surrounded the bodies to protect them from the attack.

Jeremiah lay mortally wounded as the battle continued around them. Angela covered their bodies with his shield. Hope and John stood with the others fending off attackers while Angela tearfully pled, "No, no, no, don't you do this to me ... open your eyes ... please … That Guy … open your eyes. Jeremiah, my love, it is I who is his executioner. He shall pay now for all he has done. Ezekiel's judgment comes now. Do not leave me, That Guy, for I have placed my heart in your hands."

"He is much stronger than ... he . . . seems!" Jeremiah struggled, his voice fading.

"And so am I, Jeremiah, my love. So am I!" Tears streamed down her face. She kissed him ever so gently. As she rose to do battle, she pulled both swords out, telling Jeremiah, "You had better not go dying on me now, That Guy, you and I still have some unfinished business to take care of. I will be back right back. This will only take a minute!"

Armed her swords, she stood and stared at Ezekiel with the hot fury of a thousand suns. She raised both weapons and charged into the melee, head-on toward the monster.

As Jeremiah lay next to death, he whispered the words, "My heart is ... in your hands. I love you, my angel. I ... will love and . . . be with you forever!"

CHAPTER 25

The Sacrifice

Simultaneously, the battle heated up on the other side of the portal. Rosemary, her sisters and John all stood on the steps of the church. Helen held her dagger to Faith's throat. Helen pointed again to the swirling sky above as the flaming chariot drew near.

"You see! She comes just as I said she would. Isn't she HOT! Your Hope is dead and now you are about to lose your Faith! So goes Faith, so goes your world!" Helen laughed proudly, relishing in her achievements.

Rosemary placed her hands over her heart. "Hope was never dead!" Swiftly, her hands opened, emitting brilliant beams of light from her palms, blinding Helen.

"My Hope lives ... she has always been right here in our hearts and souls, right next to my Faith, who will also never leave us!"

The evil priestess shrieked out commands to Helen.

"Do away with her ... rid this world of Faith. Why do ye hesitate? Kill that witch, fool! Smite the life from her ... take her now, I say!"

"MOMMA?" Faith yelled in anguish.

Obeying the command, Helen, plunged the knife deep into Faith's neck, letting her fall to the ground. Her eyesight returned, and she looked down at the body at her feet. The body was not Faith, but her mother, Rosemary.

Esther cried out as she stood witness to her sister's demise. "No, Lord, no!"

Faith now stood in front of Helen where her mother had stood seconds before. Her bow quivered, and she aimed her arrow straight at Helen's heart.

"ROSEMARY?" Ruth yelled out her sister's name. She turned to Helen in pure anger.

"You killed my baby sister, witch!"

Tears cloud Faith's eyes. She wanted horribly to release her arrow deep into Helen's black heart. She could see above the four beasts and the evil priestess' flaming chariot stampeding closer through the portal opening. She glanced to her left. Pouring out of the heavy gray mist came screaming Moloch soldiers. They quickly surrounded the clearing and were about to pounce upon them.

"Hey, you, over here, come on, and try to kill me then! I just killed your Momma, fool! Place your arrow here! Put your arrow right here!" Helen begged, slapping her chest with one hand. "I gladly give my life so that you can witness the wrath of my princess and the death of all your loved ones! He will not answer you, nor can you be victorious today for all is already forsaken! Don't you see who is doing this?" Helen pointed up to the sky.

Rosemary's voice spoke to Faith. "Do not trust her lies, my child! Do not let anger or sorrow make your choice! Let your faith guide your arrow. Trust in your heart!"

Faith spoke final words to Helen. "I forgive you for what you have done and may God have mercy on your soul, Helen Troy, for I shall have none! Meet your death, witch!"

Faith's arrow flew and pierced right through Helen's body, pushing her higher into the air. At the pull of the bowstring, her arrows appeared. In a blink, Faith has launched two more golden arrows into the air. One of them exploded, totally blackening the sky with thousands of smaller arrows. They rained down on the Moloch soldiers with precision, striking those threatening John and her aunts. Her continuous hailstorm of arrows poured down nonstop on the evil Moloch army marching out of the mist.

The other arrow glowed ice blue as it whistled upwards toward the black hole in the clouds to intercept its target, the blazing red witch.

Ruth heard Rosemary's voice speak to her as clear as day, "Sister ... blow that horn and keep blowing it as long and hard as you can!"

"I hear you, Sister Rose, I hear you!" Looking at Rosemary lying dead on the ground, Ruth wet her lips, closed her eyes and took her deepest breath. She blew into the golden ram's horn with all her might. From the horn came the most beautiful symphony of sounds. The heavenly music brought forth a reckoning.

Esther held her niece's bibles in her hand. They magically rose, pages ripping and taking flight on their own. One book's pages formed into a spinning tornado. They spun and spun, gathering more and more speed and velocity, hurling ahead of the ice blue arrow toward the tunnel of time. The pages of the other tore away and tumbled across the ground, each landing on a separate grave in the cemetery. Righteous warriors spill out of each grave, charging into battle.

Through the portal, the evil army advanced toward Easter's hidden place beneath the pulpit. Hope shouted over to the reverend.

"Reverend, the cross . . . I need the cross! Throw it to me, then ring the bell! It must be you who tolls the bell!"

Reverend Bishop, fighting valiantly, pulled the cross from his waist and threw it with all his might over to Hope. In mid-air, the cross changed into John's golden, double-edged sword and fell directly into Hope's hand. A surprisingly agile Reverend Bishop jumped up, grabbing onto the rope of the steeple bell. He swung above the battle, bouncing up and down. The bell rang softly at first. With sword in hand, he continued cutting down his attackers with every downswing as the bell built up momentum, ringing loudly.

The fiercest battle still raged between Angela and Ezekiel. Angela's strength grew stronger as the beautiful musical sounds of the horn blew through the portal, combining with the ringing of the bell.

The evil Ilesha had almost reached the end of the portal when her beasts stopped, caught up in the whirling pages of the bible. Faith's other glowing arrow shattered into a steel wall of arrows, preventing the evil priestess' entrance into the future. In her frantic attempt to turn around, the flaming chariot flipped over. The flaming priestess tumbled weightlessly and uncontrollably in the volatile portal. She grabbed hold of one of the fleeing beasts. Her fate depended on escaping the time vortex.

Overwhelming Ezekiel, Angela swords began to glow. She yelled, *"I AM YOUR EXECUTIONER!"* In a double blow of blinding speed, she cut off both of his arms. She spun around him, reappearing behind. Plunging both her glowing swords into him just as he had done to her Jeremiah, she impaled him. She lifted the gargantuan beast with on two swords high above her head. She walked around in a circle displaying his demise to all his cringing evil followers. She slammed his lifeless body to the ground. It burned and then vanished.

The names of every Negro Union soldier who died began to burn into the white crosses behind the church. Soldiers materialized, dressed in the armor of blue and gold. Reinforcements of fallen soldiers from wars past began to rise from the graves to fill the ranks. The clouds above rumbled in synchrony with the earth below.

With a deadly quickness, they attacked the Moloch soldiers and monster beasts. Soon the whole clearing became a battlefield. The soldiers swiftly overpowered the evil, driving them back into the foggy woods.

* * *

In the future, evil was losing the battle against the righteous also, and fading in into the woods.

Still alive, Helen transformed into her demonic form. Silently, she slithered through the grass like a snake toward Faith, who was concentrating on the evil priestess, still trying to escape through the other end of the vortex. John panicked, seeing Helen behind Faith, holding the long, curved dagger in her hand.

"Helen lives!" Using all his strength, he yanked out his rusty, heavy sword and flung it end over end in an attempt to stop Helen's deadly strike. Helen dropped to the ground.

John screamed, "Faith, watch out!"

Faith quickly turned, right into the path of the rusty sword meant for Helen, killing her instantly.

"Oh, my God, no no no ... what have I done?" John screamed in horrid agony, covering his face.. Faith's dead body lay next to Helen, who turned and smiled at John.

"It is done, Father! I come to you now." Her body went up in flames and disappeared. John opened his eyes to see Faith as he saw Hope the day she died in the last battle. She glowed with a radiant pale blue color. Faith rose up toward the bellowing funnel with her bow and arrow in hand. John fell to his knees in grief. He placed his face in his hands and began to weep.

At that same moment, a glowing brilliant pale blue aura covered Hope. She rose above the battle with the child, Easter, in her arms, flying over everyone and placing the child into the protective arms of Angela. Hope flew up toward the black portal above and shouted to her sister.

"Here I come ... I'm coming, Faith!"

They both stood at the openings on either end of the black time portal.

Faith smiled at seeing her sister standing at the other end of the portal. They waved at each other and made funny gestures, mocking the priestess' dilemma. Hope advised the evil spirit.

"You're not going to make it, you know." Hope's voice calmly floated down the abyss.

Both waved their weapons triumphantly, and both watched as the whirlwind carrying the pages from the bible engulfs the evil flaming priestess.

"No, no, do not let it end this way!" the evil priestess begged. "It must not end this way, it cannot end this way please . . . you promised me immortality . . . don't let them SHUT ME IN HERE!" she screamed like a banshee at the two twins. "This will not rid you of us, YOU ignorant NIGG—" Before she could finish, the vortex linking the past and the future imploded, producing a beautiful rainbow.

Hearing the flaming woman's last attempt at slander, Ruth turned to her sister with a sour frown and asked, "I *know* she wasn't about to use the 'N' word, was she, Esther?"

"Sure did sound like it to me!" Esther replied, scornfully spitting on the ground in disgust.

CHAPTER 26

"The Gift"

Rain began to pour down on both worlds. Those that were evil screamed and cursed in pain and torment as their bodies liquefied under the relentless downpour. The dead bodies melted away, disposing of the evil wounded and the ones left behind. The few remaining disappeared into the foggy woods, screaming in terror for mercy.

For Jeremiah, along with the other righteous ones injured in battle, the rain graced their bodies, making them whole and new again. The heavenly rain squelched out the fire burning the church, raising it like a phoenix from the ashes, totally restored. The stained glass windows and the carvings on the pews now reflected the battles that took place there, past and future.

In the present, the rain restored all the death and destruction Helen caused with all her conjured natural catastrophes, washing away memories as if nothing had ever occurred. It was a new day that proved dreams and miracles do come true, if you have enough hope and faith in them, anything was possible.

For those gathered at the Church of God in the Mariah of the past, the Reverend Bishop and Jeremiah looked on with respect as each soldier returned to their gravesites. Each one looked with pride at their names burned into the white wooden grave markers. They looked with graciousness to the angel, Hope, now standing with Angela. Before returning to their eternal rest, the fallen soldiers snapped to attention, saluting the Reverend, Jeremiah, John, Hope, and Angela, happily returning to their newly marked gravesites.

Hope turned to Angela and held her hand out.

"It is time for us to return also!"

"I am ready!" Angela sadly responded. She placed Easter into Jeremiah's arms. The child began to whimper. Jeremiah, tearing up himself, held the child.

A blue aura shone next to them. Faith suddenly appeared before them, standing beside her sister. She took Angela's hand.

"As promised you in your mortal life, your reward would come and bring That Guy of your dreams to you! You are gifted with a new purpose here now."

She took Jeremiah's hand into hers.

"This is your reward for your unbending faith, Angela. You are to stay here in Mariah as a mortal woman with Jeremiah and the child at your side. You are to raise and take care of Easter as her mortal guardians, for you both have served well without compromise."

Faith joined Angela and Jeremiah's hands together, giving a special blessing to their Holy Matrimony. "This union is made with God's blessing. Always keep Hope and Faith alive within yourselves. Always know we are right here whenever needed." She placed her hands on Angela's chest, above her heart, then on Jeremiah's, and finally on Easter's.

The angelic twins smiled joyfully at the newlyweds and rose into the heavens above, fading away in a brilliant glow of blue light.

* * *

In the future, the battle over, Ruth and Esther stood together amazed, seeing their sister Rosemary still alive. She explained to them what was really going on.

"Sisters, I died a few hours ago upstairs in my room at home. My spirit has been here with you since. It is time now to leave this earth and go home, sisters. Faith and Hope wait for us with everyone else. Our souls are old and long in need of eternal rest. When the day does come again, as it surely will, somebody is going to have a lot of explaining to do."

Esther commented, "Well, that closes the book on it all!"

"Not quite! What about him?" Ruth asked bitterly, referring to John.

Rosemary's expression suddenly changed to a solemn one. She looked unemotionally over at John, who was sitting mumbling, grieving, having removed his sword from Faith's neck. He rocked back and forth on the ground, holding Faith's dead body cradled in his arms, unaware. She spoke to her sisters, not taking her eyes off John.

"He is part of the reason I returned. There is one last purpose to fulfill before I take my leave from this earth. Prepare, for we will be leaving directly."

"John!" Rosemary's voice calmly spoke out in harmony with the voices of her daughters. Surprised, John looked up. Rosemary stood at the top of the stairs in front of the church. Tears streamed down her face.

"Oh God, Rosemary I am so sorry! Look at what I have done! I tried my best. I failed to protect your daughters and keep them safe from harm. Why, Rosemary? Why did he take both of them from me? Just like my Mother and Father!"

Rosemary listened without compassion.

"I didn't mean to kill her. I was trying to save her from Helen."

"Bring my baby here to me, John."

John carried Faith's body up to the top of the church stairs, laying her at Rosemary's feet.

"The witch set me up to kill Faith. I was trying to stop her from stabbing Faith in the back. I failed you Rosemary—I failed, I failed." John whimpered, his voice full of sorrow and self-pity.

She looked down on him and with a cold calmness, said, "Isn't it all a little too late for that, John? I am a spirit. I passed away hours ago. I returned with a gift John, the gift of knowledge. The same gift Angela, Hope and Faith possessed. All know what you have kept hidden. How many times did you turn your back on the opportunity to seek your atonement? To face your sins? How many times did someone beg and warn you to do the right thing? You never did confess all your true secrets and sins, did you, John!"

John stared coldly into Rosemary's eyes. "I did confess! You were sitting right there! I did leave out when I tried to commit murder and kill the sheriff thinking it might bring back my mom and dad. But that didn't count, he was a Moloch! I told her that I fell back in love with Hope! Heck, Rosemary, we were in the year 1867! I did not know how or if I was ever coming back here again!"

She stared back at him with an unsympathetic eye. John then blurted out, "Is this my penance, Rosemary, for loving both of your daughters? Blamed for simply being a mortal man, too weak with love for the both of them to make a choice?" he shouted angrily.

"Who are you trying to convince of your innocence, John … yourself? What goes around always comes back around. You should understand all of this by now. You were to confess *all* that you had done to Faith, but you could not do that … could you. You still refuse to admit the truth. Isn't that right … Mr. Thomas Delroy!"

Her mention of his false name sent shockwaves through John's body and mind. Giving Rosemary an evil stare, he became terribly distraught as she continued to speak the truth.

"You knew you became lost to your hatred and vengeance the night of your parents' death, even more so after losing your virginity to that innocent girl in the town of Odem, posing as Thomas Delroy. Then you had the poor pregnant woman killed when she tried to make her way down here for safety.

"Oh, yes, I know of your young pregnant woman, Ernestine Jackson. I know that you murdered her. Consumed by your hatred, you turned and became one of them soon after your parents died. In a moment of weakness, evil placed Ernestine and you under a spell and you both became part of a diabolical plan. Knowing the baby that Ernestine brought into this world was your child, you summoned Joppa to kill them. You fell down and never got up, John.

The revelation ripped off John's mask of deceit.

A year and a half ago marked the first time he'd left Mariah alone, traveling to the town of Odem, Massachusetts. John had the chance encounter with the beautiful spunky, flirtatious, Ernestine Jackson in the sleazy bar on the beach. Already brought there under evil's spell, her resemblance to his beloved twins was so remarkable, she could have been a their triplet sister. A temptation impossible to resist, under evil's spell, he lied to her about everything—his name, his work, and where he lived, in order to get with her.

Rosemary's distant voice brought John back to the moment of reality.

"It's time to go!" She closed her eyes and bowed her head in prayer.

Helen's long knife materialized next to John's bended knees. He saw the reflection of his eyes turned grey in the blade beneath him. A look of dire panic covered his face, as John's eyes flamed up and Ezekiel's evil repossessed his soul and body. He grabbed the knife and turned to attack, too late—Rosemary already striking down with Faith's golden double-edged sword, swiftly severing his head from his body.

"Forgive him. May the Lord have mercy on his soul!" she prayed.

Rosemary tossed the sword to the ground and solemnly walked back over to her sisters.

"Hmmph, hummph, humph. Well, I'll be! Who would have thought? I knew there was something wrong the minute I touched him," Esther commented.

"I thought I caught a whiff of the evil in him when he first walked into your house, Rosemary!" Ruth confessed.

Rosemary summed it up with a solemn testimony. "We all must reap what we sew. What goes around always comes back around. In time and on time, Amen. Come on, it is time for us to leave this place; everybody's up there waiting for us. Let's go!" They all held hands, giggling like they did as children growing up in Mariah. The sisters lay in the long grass, closing their eyes and passing in their sleep. Their bodies began to glow a pale blue and faded away.

CHAPTER 27

The Christmas Card

I t was a beautiful spring day in the city of Boston. A midday doorbell ring brought a special delivery to the Jackson household. The Postmaster General from the town of Odem nervously stood at the Jackson's front door, making this a very personal, very special, delivery. Five months had passed since the tragic death of their daughter, Ernestine Jackson.

Girard answered the door.

"Hello, Mr. Jackson? The United States Post Office sends the most humble apologies and extends its condolences for your loss, sir. I hear her artwork is quite a collector's item these days." The Postmaster handed him a Christmas card. "Again, I am so sorry for your loss and the delay in our delivery." With a sad tip of his hat, he delivered the beautiful Christmas card home to its final destination.

Girard admired the precious envelope, recognizing Ernestine's matchless artwork. It stood alone as one of the most beautiful handcrafted pieces of art his daughter ever composed. Choking up in grief, he covered his mouth, barely able to hold back the tears swelling in his eyes. He whispered to himself as he clears his eyes and throat, "I can't let Dorothy see me crying!"

Girard got it together and slowly walked to the back porch, stopping at the screen door, sadly watching his wife for a few moments. She was sitting in her swing, staring blankly at her once-beautiful backyard garden she had not touched all spring. She attempted to tend the yard every day; however, she ended up spending all her time just sitting, rocking in the swing, mourning her daughter.

"How you feeling today, honey?" He closely watched her, speaking from inside the screened-in porch.

"I'm okay, I guess, dear!" Dorothy sighed deeply. "Was that the doorbell I heard?" she asked, looking off distantly.

Girard stepped out into the backyard, walking toward her with the unopened letter in hand.

"Yes, Dottie ... it was the Postmaster from Odem. He personally drove down to deliver a lost letter … it's a Christmas card … from Ernestine, dear!"

"From Ernestine, you say? Oh, my Lord!" She covered her open mouth in silent wonderment as tears immediately swelled in her eyes. They sat together crying for long minutes, admiring their daughter's amazingly detailed piece of artwork. Anxious as to what the letter said, Girard he opened it.

He pointed to the post date.

"Look, she wrote this a few days before——!"

He stopped short, choosing not to talk about their daughter's last days seeing the look of gloom instantly cover his wife's face.

"I don't think I can read it right now, Girard," Dorothy admitted, shutting her tearful eyes. He took her hand. They sat holding the letter together. Moments passed.

"How about we go ahead and read it?" He gave her some encouragement, pecking her on the cheek. Dorothy, squeezing his hand, gave him a little sad smile.

Nodding, she carefully took out the card. "Let's look at this beautiful card first!"

They admired the breathtaking metallic mixture of bronze and copper on a hand-painted portrait of a golden winged angel in flight. The reflecting light caused the image of the angel to flutter across the front of the card as if it were truly flying.

Dottie took a deep breath, releasing a light sigh, and cuddled under her husband's arm.

"Okay, I'm ready now, dear! Go ahead and read it."

Making sure she was comfortable, he began.

> December 21, 2014
> Merry Christmas, My Dearest Momkiee and Dat-tee:
>
> I hope this letter finds you blessed and in good health. I love and miss you both so very much. I am blessed and doing fine. You will be happy to hear that I have found and joined a wonderful Baptist church here in town named the Church of God. I have been

attending services regularly and going to Bible school every Wednesday. (Can you believe that, Mama!)

The Good Pastor, Jeremiah Stone, re-baptized me after hearing my confessions. I am very proud to tell you that I am now born once again. I know Daddy will be glad to hear that!

Not in school this winter session, not to worry, I am keeping busy with my greeting cards. The business is doing great and has really picked up during this holiday season. I needed a break before starting my senior semester anyway!

Momma, be sure to tell Daddy I spend a lot of time in fellowship and doing volunteer work at the church. Can you believe your daughter is now a devout church member? Ha-ha!☺

Anyway, this is just a short note to tell you how much I love and miss you both dearly. I look forward to seeing you and I have a big surprise and so much to share when I visit you both on Christmas! Give each other a kiss and a big hug for me! With all my love, can't wait to get there and see you! God bless you both.

God is always with us and so is my love.

Your Loving Daughter,
Ernestine

Reading the card brought back life and happiness into their dark, tragedy-stricken home. The letter lifted Dorothy and Jerry's spirits from their grieving sorrow and suffering pain. They turned, hearing a young girl's playful voice shouting in the yard next door. It made them think of their young Ernestine.

"Woohooo! Who wants candy?" the young girl shouted and quickly darted off, holding candy canes high in the air. The other kids chased after her, yelling and screaming in joy. Off in the faint distance the fading joyful voice let go a loud rambunctious, "Wooo hooooo!"

A pleasant smile spread across Dorothy's face. She put on her sunbonnet, and got up humming. She walked in the sun over to her garden and began to till the soil.

Girard, ecstatic at seeing his wife working in the garden with a brightened spirit, got up, laughing aloud.

"Now that's what I'm talking about, Dottie! Let me help you, dear!"

CHAPTER 28

The Big Payback

I n the woods near the clearing of the church, the quiet engine purred out of the black dubbed-out Chevy truck. Sitting in the front seat, the twins stared hungrily at the driver then turned and looked at each other with furled, brooding eyebrows.

The driver, hunched over the steering wheel and rocking back and forth, can hardly hold back the giggles as the truck hit the black top with its fancy big chrome wheels and began to speed away from the town of Mariah.

With a snap of the finger, the radio blasts on, playing "The Payback" by James Brown.

"Whew wee, what in hell is that smell? It's smelling worse than a dead man's ass in August up in here." Reverend Bishop rolled down his window, sticking his head out and gasping for the cold fresh air.

Patience shouted to the stranger, "Mommy, where is my mommy? Humgry ... I'm hungry!" She banged her rattle angrily against the window of the truck.

"Me too, me too!" the other twin, Hope, complained, holding up two fingers, then covering her nose.

Rocking to the beat, the reverend, annoyed, looked over at the children.

Patience shook her rattle angrily at her sister as they zipped past signpost that announced they were leaving the town of Mariah.

"Stinky two, stinky two!" Hope juts her finger places the blame on her sister.

"You too, you too! Where is my mommy?" Patience screamed at Reverend Bishop, pinching her own nose.

Reverend Bishop stopped the truck, still wearing sunglasses in the pitch darkness.

"Your mommy gone bye-bye! yes . . . . yes . . . food, food. I know you need some food. We need to change those nasty diapers you all got on there first, then get something to eat, but we can't hang out around here any longer."

He finished changing their diapers and mumbled a chant. Two baby bottles appeared in their hands, filled with sherry.

"In the meantime, suck these and, oh, yeah, Merry Christmas!"

He giggled after taking a long swig himself from his flask. He took a real deep breath and choked, getting the full brunt of the horrible-smelling diapers.

"Whew wee! Look here, let's get something straight right now! I believe in cleanliness around this camp. You just are going to have hold any more crapping until we get to where we going!" He scolded the twins, dumping the two dirty diapers filled with baby poop on the side of the road.

They stared at him imagining just how sweet his heart was going to taste when they devoured him.

"Da Da?" Patience asked with an evil smirk.

"Hell, no, I ain't your damn daddy! Shut up and drink your bottles! That should put y'all right to sleep." Reverend Bishop spoke to himself. He then began to giggle under his breath, taking another swig out of his flask.

He searched the woods behind him in the rear view mirror then looked at himself. No longer recognizable, he now had long, gray dreadlocks. He giggled, taking his hand and running it along his long, gray moustache. His face wore a nappy grey beard. His left eye had turned a bluish-gray. Removing a gauze bandage from where Rosemary slapped him across his face with the frying pan, he saw a keloid scar had formed across his closed swollen right eye and down his face. His nose was broken.

He looked out his side window and began to laugh, rocking back and forth in his car seat. The reverend turned and spoke urgently in a thick southern drawl.

"We's ain't got no time to waste. We got business to, to take care of, like a little wedding reception to attend and ... and you two girls have a choir to join!

Yes, siree, we going back to Mariah, all right, and get revenge ... the big payback! So now let's go change us some history, gals!"

The music got louder and he began singing with the voice of James Brown. He giggled, rocking to the beat while the black fancy truck transformed into a covered wagon drawn by four black Arabian horses. Crammed inside sat boxes of bibles, supplies and barrels of sherry wine.

Babies no longer, two young girls now sat in the back of the wagon, their stomachs growling louder and louder with hunger. Patience looked over to Hope, both pairs of grey eyes were red with fire. In her mother's voice, she whispered under the music into her sisters' ear.

"As for the good reverend, his will be the first heart we will eat, marinated heavily in a sweet mixture of sin and religion. We will drink his hot blood and believe me, we are going to enjoy every morsel of him as if it were . . . mmmm, Heaven sent!"

Bumping their heads, grooving with the beat, they smiled at each other, enjoying the song. They gave each other silent high-fives.

The reverend, sitting up on the buckboard, stopped the music, sniffed the air. A cigar butt jutted out the corner of his mouth. He snapped, lighting up his middle finger. Magically changing into cowboy attire and fancy black snake skinned boots, he pulled his big black Stetson cowboy hat way down low so the brim covered his eyes and popped his collar to hide his face. He dragged slowly, blowing a big cloud of smoke into the air in front of them.

"Return us to Mariah!" The old black cowboy commanded.

"Yee-hah ... giddy-yap there! I got a hot date," Cracking his flaming whip in the air, the Big Payback music started up again as they began their journey back into time to Mariah. The horses neighed loudly as the covered wagon lurched forward into the flaming sphere. They all vanished leaving present-day Mariah with a heavy scent of sulfur and stinking diapers in the air. A bone-chilling laugh spread over the valley.

The End

Dedicated in loving Memory of
Ernestine Marie Wood

October 08, 1974 to December 23, 1999
You forever live in our hearts
and memories, Teeny.

ABOUT THE AUTHOR

Born in Detroit I was thirteen years old when I got my first real job I rode around the city selling farm fresh eggs and chicken as a delivery route boy off of Harold's Egg Truck. Growing up in what was then called the 'inner city' during the '50's, 60's and early 70's beats the heart and soul of my roots in the heydays and glory years of 'Motown' and the Big Three, Chrysler, Ford and General Motors. I grew up in a city filled with creative talented artist and the never give up attitude that defines the girth of the 'Motor City'. I join the ranks of the few African American Fantasy Fiction writers. I love writing spooky scary stuff on a black tip with a bump trying to make available a fresh new entrée of imagination to readers across the board.